"What've you got for me?"
Longarm asked.

Vail grunted in triumph and pulled forth a sizable folder. He glanced up at Longarm, a gleam in his eye. "I don't think you're going to mind this case one little bit," he told the lawman. "Seems you're about to go looking through all the whorehouses in Colorado for a duchess."

"A what?"

"There ain't nothin' wrong with your hearin', is there?"

"You said 'duchess.'"

"That's what I said."

Longarm shrugged, then smiled wryly. "I'm listening, chief."

TABOR EVANS

LONGARM

AND THE FRONTIER DUCHESS

A JOVE BOOK

LONGARM AND THE FRONTIER DUCHESS

A Jove Book/published by arrangement with
the author

PRINTING HISTORY
Jove edition/September 1985

ISBN: 0-515-08343-7

Jove books are published by The Berkley Publishing Group,
200 Madison Avenue, New York, N.Y. 10016. The words
"A JOVE BOOK" and the "J" with sunburst are trademarks
belonging to Jove Publications, Inc.

PRINTED IN THE UNITED STATES OF AMERICA

LONGARM

AND THE
FRONTIER DUCHESS

Chapter 1

Pausing outside the Windsor Hotel, Deputy U. S. Marshal Custis Long—known to his friends as Longarm—bent to light his cheroot. As he did so a young lady, obviously frightened, rushed around the corner and almost ran into him.

"Oh, sir!" she cried. "Please! You must help me!"

Flicking away his match, Longarm nodded quickly and touched his hatbrim to her. "Well now," he said, smiling to allay her fears, "there's no reason why I wouldn't help you, ma'am. Just tell me what it is that's bothering you."

"There's a man following me!"

Longarm took a long look at the girl. It was close on to dusk, but Longarm could see her face quite clearly. He judged her to be no more than twenty-five or -six, a right pert-looking filly with a swelling bosom under her expensive dress. Under the fashionably wide brim of her hat, he glimpsed a luxurious bounty of reddish-brown hair, a pair of sparkling blue eyes, a bold chin, and a neck long and

1

graceful. She wore no rouge. Her peaches-and-cream complexion did not need such embellishment.

"Ma'am," Longarm told her softly, his voice close to a warm chuckle, "any man in Denver who would *not* follow you would have to be blind."

She blushed crimson. "Why . . . thank you, sir," she managed. "I am sure you mean that as a compliment. But *this* man . . . !" She shuddered. *"His* attentions I certainly do not wish to attract."

"I understand, ma'am," Longarm said, looking up quickly as a man dressed in spats and dark trousers and frock coat appeared from around the corner.

Following Longarm's gaze, the girl turned. "That's him . . . !" she gasped, pointing. "He's the man!"

The fellow took one look at Longarm, turned, and vanished back around the corner.

"Maybe I'll just have a talk with him," said Longarm, leaving the girl to hurry after the fleeing masher.

It did not take long for the tall, long-legged lawman to catch up to the fellow. Grabbing his shoulder, Longarm spun him around. The fellow, a lean, cadaverous individual with frightened eyes and a receding chin, flung his arm up to protect himself from Longarm.

"My dear sir," he wailed. "What is the meaning of this?"

Longarm pushed the man none-too-gently back against a wall. The crowd filing past gave both men a wide berth, not wishing to get involved.

"Why were you chasing that woman?" Longarm demanded.

"Chasing that woman? Why, sir, I assure you, I was doing nothing of the sort."

"Then why did you run?"

"That woman you were talking to—she pointed at me and cried out!"

Longarm considered the man's reply for a long moment. The man appeared terrified, and his lower lip was trembling like that of a little boy whose hand had just been caught in the cookie jar. He made a somewhat pathetic masher, if that was what he was.

"Do you know who I am?" Longarm demanded.

"Her . . . her husband?"

Longarm laughed and flung the man from him. "Keep away from her!"

The fellow scurried off like a whipped cur.

Longarm watched him go for a moment, then turned and walked back to the young lady.

"He thought I was your husband, ma'am. I don't think he'll be bothering you any more tonight."

She took a deep breath. "I don't know how to thank you, Mr. . . . ?"

"Long," he told her, bowing gallantly. "Custis Long."

"And I am Miss Rosemary Sutcliff," she replied, extending her gloved hand. "I am pleased to meet you, Mr. Long—and very grateful."

Longarm took her hand in his and shook it gently. "Won't you step into the hotel, Rosemary, and join me in a glass of wine? It might help to settle your nerves some."

"You are very kind, Mr. Long. As a matter of fact, I am staying at this very hotel, and a glass of wine with a real gentleman would do much, I am sure, to erase the memory of this most disagreeable experience."

It took some time for the wine to erase her displeasure completely, and as Longarm sat across from her in the shadowed booth well away from the smoke-filled saloon on the other side of the dining room, he found himself drawn to this blue-eyed damsel. So dark blue were her eyes, in fact, that they were almost purple, and she pulsed with a vital, animal energy that sent the juices surging through him at a

3

reckless pace. He could sense she was just as attracted to him.

Rosemary was from Dorsetshire, England, which did not surprise Longarm. Her accent and the fine precision of her words had told him that at once. Though he probed gently at her reason for journeying this far into the American West, she told him little of her mission, beyond mentioning that she was hoping to find a very dear friend soon. For his part, Longarm kept his own occupation to himself. Women, he had found, were sometimes repelled at the nature of his employment—the nature and the uncertainty of it.

The evening passed swiftly and Rosemary was quite agreeable to having Longarm escort her upstairs to her room. Yet the moment he turned the key in her door and pushed it open, she kissed his cheek lightly and slipped quickly past him. Plucking the key deftly from his hand, she vanished into her room with a dazzling smile and closed the door quietly but firmly, leaving Longarm standing there with only the memory of her smile to comfort him.

Chuckling at her adroit escape, Longarm tipped his hat to the door, reached for a cheroot, and left the hotel.

The next morning, feeling slightly undone by all that wine, Longarm strode swiftly up Colfax on his way to the federal courthouse. A tall, raw-boned man, he moved with a speed and grace that was almost spooky to some. He wore low-heeled cavalry stovepipes he had molded to his feet and which enabled him to cover distance afoot considerably faster than would have been possible in regular riding boots. Dressed as usual in his brown tweed pants, vest and frock coat, his woolen shirt was a gunmetal gray, and at his throat he had knotted a black shoestring tie. He wore his snuff-brown Stetson dead center and tilted slightly forward, cavalry style, the crown telescoped in the Colorado rider's fashion. This was a legacy from his youth when he had run away to ride in the War. Longarm preferred to "dis-remember" which side he had fought for, since it didn't pay a man to talk too much about that past unpleasantness between the Blue and the Gray—not out here in Colorado, at any rate.

Beneath the brim of his hat Longarm's face appeared as dark and weather-worn as an Indian's. But the gunmetal blue of his wide-set eyes and the tobacco-leaf color of his close-cropped hair gave indisputable evidence of his Anglo-Saxon birth—that and the flaring longhorn mustache he favored. Beneath the mustache, his mouth was wide and expressive, his square lantern jaw solid and powerful.

Longarm was fully armed, but not a trace of it showed. Under the left side of his frock coat, his cross-draw rig carried a Colt Model T .44-40, the barrel cut down to five inches and the front sight filed off as useless scrap that could only hang up in his open-toed holster. In addition to the Colt, Longarm carried a little surprise in the right breast pocket of his vest: a double-barrelled .44 derringer, the brass butt of which was attached to a gold-washed chain and that in turn to the Ingersoll watch he kept in his left vest pocket.

He kept his silver federal badge inside his wallet and an extra handful of cartridges in the right-side pocket of his coat. His other pocket carried a bundle of waterproof matches and a pair of handcuffs. The key to his cuffs and his room were in his left pants pocket along with his jackknife.

As he strode along, aware that he was late—as usual—those crowding the sidewalk gave way instantly to this tall, intent man obviously in his prime. Barely aware of the scurrying city-bred townsfolk darting out of his path, Long-arm swept in, his mind still on that auburn-haired damsel with the bright blue eyes who had so neatly outmaneuvered him the night before.

He was hoping to meet her again, perhaps at the Windsor Hotel that evening.

Reaching the steps of the courthouse, he hurried inside and elbowed his way through a crowd of waxen-faced lawyers and other dudes smelling of macassar hair oil. Swiftly striding up a marble staircase, he made his way to a large oak door with gold lettering on it which read: UNITED STATES MARSHAL, FIRST DISTRICT COURT OF COLORADO.

Pushing inside, he saw a pale, lank-haired clerk seated at the rolltop desk. Leaving off his pounding on the newfangled writing machine they called a typewriter, the clerk turned and grinned maliciously up at Longarm.

"Mr. Vail's been out here twice lookin' for you," he said.

"My, my, sonny," Longarm replied as he strode past him and pushed his way through the low gate. "Why, that's enough to make a grown man tremble."

Pausing only long enough to knock once on the chief's door, Longarm pushed it open and entered Marshal Billy Vail's office.

"So there you are," growled the marshal from behind his desk. "Where the hell have you been? It's almost eight-thirty!"

"Sorry, chief," Longarm replied, slipping into the morocco leather chair across the desk from his superior. "What've you got for me?"

Vail sighed and stared morosely at him for a long moment, then gave it up as a bad job. It was, he knew, useless to chew out Longarm, though that didn't mean he wasn't always ready to give it a try. "Well, for one thing," Vail replied, commencing to paw through the drifts of folders, letters, and dodgers on his desk, "it looks like I finally got an assignment that should get you out of Denver—and out of my hair—for a good long spell."

Longarm's eyebrows canted. Vail's words pleased him.

As usual, he was getting pretty damned tired of this grimy, mile-high dung heap, and he had been complaining long and hard at the nickel-and-dime assignments Vail had been sending him on these past couple of weeks. Taking out a cheroot, he lit it, then leaned back and gazed at the banjo clock on the oak-paneled wall while he waited for Vail to find the folder he had misplaced.

When his eyes lit finally on the aging federal marshal, Longarm could not help noticing how pale and flabby Vail looked. In his day, Marshal Vail had shot it out with the Comanche, the Kiowa, assorted owlhoots, and—to hear him tell it—half of Mexico. He didn't look it now, though. He was balding and turning to suet, and every time Longarm took a good look at his chief, he took it as a grim reminder of what his own fate might be if he did not stay away from towns and desks.

At last Vail grunted in triumph and pulled forth a sizable folder. He glanced up at Longarm, a gleam in his eye. "I don't think you're going to mind this case one little bit," he told the lawman. "Seems you're about to go looking through all the whorehouses in Colorado for a duchess."

"A what?"

"There ain't nothin' wrong with your hearin', is there?"

"You said 'duchess.'"

"That's what I said."

Longarm shrugged, then smiled wryly. "I'm listening, chief."

"I have here a letter from the State Department in Washington," Vail said impressively, "and it contains the good news that Queen Victoria herself also wants action." Vail grinned demonically. "So I guess you could say you're working for Queen Victoria as well as the State Department on this one."

Longarm stirred restlessly in his seat and chewed down

on the end of his cheroot. "Get on with it, chief."

Vail dropped the folder on the desk in front of him and leaned back in his chair. "Well, first off, this here duchess everyone wants us to find wasn't a duchess until a little while ago."

"You want to explain that?"

"Her brother was the Duke of Clyde. Along with his wife and children, the duke died in a yachting accident in the North Sea—so now the title goes to her. Thing is, she's so busy whoring her way through the New World, she don't have no idea that she's had a change in fortune."

"And I'm supposed to find her."

"That's the ticket, Longarm. And maybe you could clean her up some while you're at it, even if you can't reform her. The main thing is to get the duchess back on the track to Merry Old England with as much of her reputation buried as you can manage. I don't figure Queen Victoria would take kindly to a duchess who's spent most of her time in America on her back."

"What's her name?"

"Jane-Marie Darnsforth."

"Is that the name she's using?" Longarm asked.

"Nope."

"Do you know what it is?"

"I'm not sure. The one she used in New Orleans was Sarah Jones. But she left New Orleans under a cloud, you might say—and there's no doubt she's changed it since."

"What is she doing this far west in the first place?"

"She got herself in a nasty scrape back in England. A gent who was supposed to marry her pulled out, leaving her reputation in tatters. So she brained him with a slops jar. She left him bleeding and smelling like hell. She was sure she had killed him, and she fled the country. The poor bastard survived, though; but she don't know that. Mean-

8

while, she's been making a living of sorts for herself in various parlor houses throughout the West. The last word we have on her put her in a place north of her called Bent Creek—a mining camp that's since gone broke."

Longarm nodded. "I know the place."

"I figure there's a good chance she's workin' Leadville now. It's really boomin' since they made that new strike."

"There's also a good chance she could be in any other boom town or cattle town north, east, or west of us."

"You got a point, Longarm," Vail admitted grudgingly.

"Do you have a picture of her?"

Vail dug into the folder and withdrew a small faded photograph. He tossed it across the desk to Longarm. Longarm picked it up and found himself looking at the smiling face of a pretty girl of nineteen or twenty. She was standing in a sunlit garden and had on a long dress and was holding a parasol to keep off sun. All Longarm could tell for sure about her was that she was pretty enough and had long, blond hair.

Longarm shook his head. "This ain't much of a picture. How long ago was it taken?"

"About five years ago, I'd say."

"Hell, Vail, this is practically worthless. Can't you get a better picture than this?"

"We were lucky to get that one. Her brother destroyed all the pictures of her he could get his hand on after she brained that gent she was goin' to marry. It was he who gave her the money for the passage to America—on the condition that she disappear for good."

"Sounds like a real gentleman."

"Oh, he was that, all right."

"I need more to go on, chief, unless you want me to visit every whorehouse west of the Mississippi. It'll take awhile, I wager. And I ain't so sure this filly is going to be very anxious to confide in me, even if I do manage to find her. She's still wanted for murder as far as she knows, so she won't be all that eager to confide in a deputy U. S. marshal. She might even try to brain me like she did her boyfriend."

"Longarm, you are too modest. You don't have any trouble with women."

"Maybe so, but I'm not all that familiar with whores, Billy."

"My, aren't you a bit peevish this morning."

Longarm shook his head wearily. "If you're serious about me trackin' this filly, you'll have to give me more help than you've given me so far."

"What, specifically?"

"Hell, I'll have to be able to recognize her, first off. Like I just said, that picture you showed me is no help at all. What I need is someone who knows her—a relative maybe, or a friend from England."

Vail smiled and got to his feet. "If that is the kind of help you need, that is the kind of help you will get." Suddenly grinning from ear to ear, he skirted his desk, opened the door, and said something Longarm could not quite catch to the clerk outside.

Then Vail returned to his desk and slumped back into his chair, an expectant gleam in his eye. A moment later the clerk opened the door, stepped to one side, and Rosemary Sutcliff swept into the office.

She was as surprised to see Longarm as he was to see her. As the clerk closed the door behind her, she pulled to a halt in some confusion.

Vail got quickly to his feet, Longarm following suit. "Come in! Come in, Miss Sutcliff!" Vail cried. "I want you to meet Mr. Long. He's the deputy I told you about—the one who's going to help you find Miss Darnsforth."

10

Longarm had his hat in his hand and a broad grin on his face as he bowed to Rosemary, aware once again of her flashing smile and dark blue eyes. If this was the friend who was going to help him track the errant duchess, he couldn't have asked for a more interesting or exciting companion.

Now he understood the gleam in Vail's eyes.

Chapter 2

As the train rattled out of Denver on its way to Leadville, Rosemary explained to Longarm how she had come to be in Denver. It seemed she had been on Jane-Marie's trail all the way from New York, having left England only a month before.

A lifelong friend of Jane-Marie's, Rosemary was intent on doing all she could to find her good friend, just as she had done what she could earlier to save Jane-Marie from the anger of her brother, and from the consequences of her violent response of her fiancé's rejection. It was Rosemary who had prevailed upon the duke to secure passage for Jane-Marie to New York, Rosemary herself who gave Jane-Marie a sum large enough to support her for a few months at least in the New World.

Though it had been Rosemary's intention to follow Jane-Marie to New York, Rosemary's family was so opposed to her doing so that they had kept her a virtual prisoner until a little more than a month ago, when Rosemary and her family learned of the death of Jane-Marie's brother. Only then, a full two years after Jane-Marie's flight, was Rosemary allowed to book passage for New York to seek out her friend.

Longarm took out a cheroot and asked permission to light up. Then he glanced at Rosemary. "When did you learn Jane-Marie had not injured her fiancé all that bad?"

"A week after I saw Jane-Marie off."

"She was in no danger of the authorities by then. Why didn't you cable her in New York?"

"I did not have her address. And she did not write me for more than a year, just as she was leaving New York for New Orleans. That was how I got her New Orleans address."

"You wrote her then and told her she was no longer wanted by the police?"

"Of course."

"What response did you get?"

"None."

"How do you account for that?"

"When I reached the house where she was working in New Orleans, I found my letter. It had not been delivered to her. She had left before it came. The madam did not have any forwarding address for Jane-Marie."

Longarm nodded and puffed a while on his cheroot. "You say you went to school with Jane-Marie?"

"Yes, a private finishing school in Dorsetshire. St. Thomas's. We both attended it since we were seven."

"By the time all this happened, you two must have been very close."

"We were like sisters. Jane-Marie was—and still is— my closest friend. You must find her, Longarm. Not just because she's now a duchess, but because she cannot go on like this, destroying herself in this fashion."

"You say you visited the house where she worked in New Orleans?"

"Yes."

"Not a very nice place, was it?"

"On the contrary. It was actually quite spacious, a very cheerful home in an elegant neighborhood. There was plenty of room for the girls, and each of them was granted quite a bit of privacy. In some ways," she said, glancing slyly at Longarm, "it resembled a very fine home I remember visiting once as a girl in Dorsetshire. The madam seemed quite enlightened. She had a policy of not overworking her best girls so, for most of them, I imagine, the life must have been quite pleasant ... I suppose." She glanced quickly at Longarm. "Of course, not that anything so degrading could be considered pleasant."

Longarm smiled. "I understand what you meant, Rosemary. I guess Jane-Marie landed in a parlor house a cut above the average. Any reason why she left?"

"It was one of the customers. His demands were ... well, unhealthy is the best way to describe them. The madam, however, seemed to think that this customer should have anything he wanted, since he was paying."

"And Jane-Marie disagreed."

"Yes."

"She didn't bash this fellow with a loaded chamber pot too, did she?"

Rosemary shuddered. "No. She just refused to stay with him that night and walked out."

"She must have had some money saved."

"Yes. One of the girls who was still there told me Jane-Marie had been saving tips on the side, keeping it in a stocking under one of the floorboards in a corner of her room. She had amassed quite a sum, according to the girl."

Longarm nodded. Evidently Jane-Marie was not the usual

innocent from abroad. In more ways than one. Very few parlor girls ever managed to stash away enough money to declare their independence.

"And what brought you to Denver?" Longarm asked.

"The girl told me Jane-Marie was heading for Denver." Rosemary leaned her head back and sighed. "So I followed her here and found the place where she had stayed. It was not a very nice place, Longarm. Aunt Sally's, it was called."

Longarm knew the parlor house. Rosemary was right. It would sure as hell represent a comedown from the New Orleans parlor house Rosemary had described.

"But when I got to it," Rosemary continued, "Jane-Marie was gone. That was when I learned she might be in Leadville."

"So you got tired of all this traipsing around and went to see Marshal Vail."

"Yes. I went to our local police first, and they referred me to him. That was when I learned that your State Department was also looking for Jane-Marie."

"Our State Department and your Majesty's government."

She nodded. "I should have realized. The College of Heralds must be very anxious to clear this matter up."

"The College of Heralds?"

"Yes. They're the men in charge of such matters. In the event the younger as well as the elder children of a peer die without issue, the College of Heralds searches for the nearest relative to whom they might award the title."

"So if they don't find Jane-Marie, it will go to someone else—a distant relative, perhaps?"

"Yes. So, you see, for Jane-Marie's sake, we must hurry."

Longarm nodded. "How much time do you think we have?"

"Not more than a month or two, I should say."

Longarm considered a moment, then shrugged. With

Rosemary along, he should have little difficulty in finding the lost duchess. He tipped his hat forward and leaned his head back against the hard, dusty back of his coach seat. The train ride to Leadville would take another four hours at least, and as soon as he could after their arrival, Longarm intended to make some discreet inquiries in some very indiscreet saloons and bawdy houses.

It was not going to be an easy task. Leadville was still going full blast. It probably had the largest per capita population of whores in North America and was a magnet for all those seeking to practice the oldest profession. It didn't seem to make any difference how many of them died alone and broke after brief lives of violence, drunkenness, and misery; there always seemed to be a perfect scramble to fill their places.

Despite all this, as Longarm knew from previous visits, prostitution was an accepted business enterprise in what they called Cloud City, the only mining town in the West which seemed to take a real civic pride in its depravity. One newspaper editor had proclaimed proudly that there were more than two hundred prostitutes in the brothels on State Street alone. And this, of course, made no allowance for the streetwalkers and the parlor houses.

No, it would not be easy, and it would not be pleasant—searching through the alleys and houses for a lost duchess.

Meanwhile, the description Rosemary had already given him of Jane-Marie had fixed with Longarm a mental portrait of a young woman whose figure was already voluptuous at seventeen, one who possessed bold, full lips, hair the color of corn silk, and large pale blue eyes. Rosemary had been at pains to point out as well that even though at first glance Jane-Marie had the look of one who might need protection and indeed was capable of arousing the most protective feelings in men, her temperament was entirely the opposite

17

of what her looks inspired. She was a willful, passionate seductress, as changeable as the wind—a personality as elusive as any Rosemary had known.

Longarm shook his head in contemplation of such a woman. From the look of it, Jane-Marie also had a character strong enough to defy a king—or the madam of a brothel, if need be. With that in mind, he was pretty certain he would not find Jane-Marie plying her trade as a common streetwalker or dance-hall girl. She would more than likely find a place in one of the more established and fancy parlor houses north of the red light district.

At least, that was what he hoped.

Arriving in Leadville a little before sundown, Longarm and Rosemary took a hack to the Clarendon and registered. Before they went up to their rooms, Longarm suggested they meet in the lobby for a late supper. Rosemary agreed, and Longarm went up to his room to freshen up.

The late supper was pleasant enough, after which Longarm escorted Rosemary to her room, bid her good night, then hurried downstairs and out of the hotel. He walked down Harrison Avenue to the next block and stepped into the Texas House.

The gambling house was as flashy as ever, plushly furnished, and as garish as any New Orleans parlor house. Waving off a frail, snaggle-toothed beer jugger who must have been all of seventeen, Longarm pushed up to the bar and purchased a bottle of Maryland rye. Then he elbowed his way past the faro and poker tables, took up residence at a table at the rear wall, and began to drink. A band was playing at the far end of the place on a small stage and a husky-looking woman in a red gown was belting out a song about what a wonderful town Leadville was.

Shouts of pleasure and heavy applause rewarded the singer's performance, and when she had bowed off—after trading a few lusty jokes with those closest to the stage—the band took over. It was loud and enthusiastic, but that was the best that could be said of it. The piano player seemed to be hitting the keys with a hammer and the trumpet player had long since lost all track of the key. Longarm winced as he poured his second drink.

A beer juggler no more than fourteen years of age sat down at his table. She propped her elbow on the table, cupped her chin in her hand, and gazed curiously at him. Her thin, not yet full lips were painted scarlet, her wan, sallow face heavily rouged with little skill and even less care.

"You like to drink alone?" she asked.

Longarm shrugged.

The girl sighed, glanced nervously at the barkeep, saw that he was busy looking elsewhere, and relaxed. "Mind if I sit here and rest up a while? We can make like we're havin' a real nice conversation."

Longarm understood. As he filled his glass for the third time, he glanced sidelong at the girl. "What's your name?"

"Molly."

"Been here long?"

"Long enough."

"I'm looking for someone."

Molly frowned slightly and lifted her chin from her palm. She was suddenly wary. Brushing her mouse-colored hair back off her pimply forehead, she fixed him with uncertain eyes. "That so?"

"She'd be a lot older than you," Longarm told her. "In her early twenties—a tall, well-endowed blonde with blue eyes and a temper."

"Ain't many girls fit that description around here, mister. We're all lots younger. Any girl like you described would

19

be working in the parlor houses. Try Frankie Paige's house or Sallie Purple's. What's her name?"

"Her name might be Sarah Jones."

"There's a Sarah Majorski working at the Alhambra Hall. But she's a redhead." Molly smiled slightly. "And her figure's all gone to hell. She's doin' a lot of opium smokin', too. It sure ain't helped her disposition none."

Longarm went back to his drink. He was satisfied. His earlier presumption that Jane-Marie would not be working this part of town seemed to be borne out by this bar girl's testimony. He dropped a coin on the table for her, then stood up.

"I didn't scare you away none, did I, mister?"

"Nope," Longarm said. "And thanks for the conversation."

"That's all right, mister. Any time. Next time you come in here, you just ask for Molly."

Longarm touched the brim of his hat to her. "I'll do that," he said, then turned and left the Texas House.

As naked as a worm, Longarm was climbing wearily into his bed when he heard a soft knock on his door. He pulled his .44 out from under his pillow, lit the lamp on the dresser, then padded to the door on naked feet.

Resting his ear against the door, he called, "Who's there?"

"Why, it's just me, Longarm," Rosemary whispered back. "No need to be afraid."

"Ma'am, I ain't decent. I just took off my britches."

She laughed softly. "Then put something on."

Longarm went back to the bed and slipped on his pants, then returned to the door, unlocked it, and pulled it open. Rosemary hurried in, her face flushed with embarrassment.

"My word, Longarm," she cried. "You certainly took

your time! A hotel patron just walked by and saw me! Imagine what he must have thought when he saw me waiting outside your door like that."

"In Leadville, he wouldn't give it a second thought."

She laughed nervously. "Yes, I suppose so. I had forgotten where I was, I am afraid."

Longarm padded back to his bed and slid the Colt under the pillow. Then he sat back down on the edge of his bed and glanced at Rosemary. She was wearing only a robe and nightgown. From what he saw of the nightdress, it appeared to be fashioned of some expensive, gossamer material that was about as substantial as a spider's web. Her long, auburn hair was combed out and her face was shining from her bath. He did not recognize her perfume, but it was effective enough—its tantalizing scent easily bridging the few feet that separated them.

It was obvious what she was doing in his room, but Longarm knew enough not to take anything for granted. And, then again, he was exhausted.

Rosemary walked closer to Longarm, then halted. "I suppose you are wondering why I'm here."

"Yes," he lied.

"I . . . wanted to apologize for my behavior in Denver."

"I thought it was most exemplary."

"Yes, so did I."

"Well, then."

"It is just that I know you better now. You are a real gentleman, Longarm. Any woman would be proud to . . . know you better."

"You are most kind."

She sat on the edge of the bed beside him. The scent she was wearing, plus the warmth of her, was like heat emanating from a lamp, and it drew him toward her like a big fool moth. He got up and turned off the lamp.

Sitting back down beside her, he said, "It's hot enough in here without that."

"I agree," she said softly. "Where did you go?"

"To the Texas House. I wanted to look around some— get my bearings."

"And did you?" She leaned her head on his shoulder.

"Not much," he admitted. "I talked to a bar girl. She told me what I had expected. There's no sign that Jane-Marie's taken to the streets in this town. She would more than likely find a place in one of the more expensive parlor houses."

"How terrible," Rosemary murmured.

"Yes, it is not the best way to earn a living."

"Sometimes," Rosemary sighed, "a woman has no choice in the matter."

"I suppose not."

"Do you think we'll ever find her? This is such a big country."

"I don't know."

Longarm was acutely aware of her nearness by this time. His mouth had gone dry and he knew that before long he was going to have to let nature take its course. The thing was, he had to be sure that this was indeed what Rosemary wanted.

"I think maybe you'd better be getting back to your room, young lady," he told her. "I'm not going to be acting very responsible much longer."

She laughed, her voice low, seductive. "I was beginning to wonder, Custis, if there was something wrong with me."

She turned her face to his then and leaned close, her lips parting expectantly. There was no way Longarm could refuse the invitation. His lips pounced on hers and, like two passionate animals, their mouths began working furiously,

22

their tongues probing with a wantonness that brought Longarm quiveringly alive. Panting softly, Rosemary pulled back.

"Oh, dear heart, you must think me shameless."

He did, but it was a perfect match for how he felt. Swiftly he slipped off his pants. Rosemary was peeling out of her robe, and then in an instant the diaphanous gown followed it, shimmering in the darkness, to the floor. She reclined her long, pale figure back on the bed, lifting one knee, her hand moving seductively over one breast, her other cupping her pubis.

Joining her on the bed, Longarm hauled her in for a blindly aimed kiss. He caught her cheek, but she swung her moist lips to his, and again, for a long moment they lay in each other's arms, attempting to melt into one another in the dark.

His lips still cleaving to hers, he ran his free hand down the length of her body to the warm moisture between her trembling thighs. She tried to cry out between their lips as Longarm parted her knees with his own. He dropped onto her then and found himself slipping into her so easily it astonished him. Sweeping up her buttocks with his free hand, he lunged in as far as he could go. Once, twice, he thrust, driving hard and deep. And still there was more of her.

Gasping, she moved to one side. "Whatever are you waiting for?" she cried. "Oh, you must go deeper!"

Even as she spoke, her legs rose up to lock firmly around Longarm's bouncing buttocks. This seemed to do it as she almost sucked him in. He increased his pace, barely conscious of the tiny, delighted cries that broke from Rosemary's gasping mouth as he neared the end of his climax. When the tip of his erection slammed against the mouth of her womb, he lost all control and came fast.

But he stayed inside her and moved her up further onto

23

the bed for a more comfortable second coming. He took his time now, as their heaving flesh got better acquainted. Suddenly Rosemary moaned and raked her nails down his back.

"Oh, God!" she sobbed. "Oh, it's so good with you! So good!"

By this time she was responding like a she-cougar in heat, gouging his back with her nails and lifting her knees until her heels were crossed behind Longarm's neck. He was hitting bottom with every stroke now and he eased off a bit, fearful of hurting her.

But she lunged up to meet his thrusts and, in a voice he barely recognized, growled, "All of it! I want all of it inside me! Oh, it's coming again!"

This time they had a long, shuddering mutual orgasm. Suddenly she went limp, her legs uncrossing, her arms outflung upon the bed. Her head sagged to one side and it took a second or two for Longarm to realize she'd passed out. Astonished and somewhat pleased—all at the same time—he lay beside her on the bed and gently tried to revive her. After a while she regained consciousness. Looking at him, she frowned, then came alive instantly, "Oh, Longarm, you've let him come out. Please! Put him back inside!"

He looked down. To his astonishment, he was still erect. Grabbing him around the waist, she presed closer to him. He grabbed her buttocks and slammed into her. She grunted and flung herself still closer, then rolled Longarm over onto his back and mounted him.

"Don't move," she whispered. "Just grow inside me."

Longarm did as she suggested.

"Ah," she whispered happily. "There! There! I can feel it growing inside me. Oh, you're still so nice and hard. My, there certainly is a *lot* of you, isn't there."

He almost returned the compliment, but decided against it. Reaching up, he fondled her breasts, letting his big fingers flick her nipples. They became as hard as bullets in no time.

She flung her head back, letting her long curls cascade down her back, and sighed contentedly. "I do so like this, Longarm! You must think me an absolute hussy, but I don't care. You must think I had this in mind from the moment I saw you in front of that hotel."

"Didn't you?"

She hesitated, then answered roguishly, "You know damned well I did. But that first time my good sense prevailed. Women are not supposed to want such things. But I must confess, I found it impossible to deny myself once I knew you were in this hotel with me." She grinned down at him, rocking gently back and forth. "I was furious when you made no effort to escort me to my room this evening. And then you went out to a saloon—leaving me alone here!"

"So now you're going to punish me?"

"Yes. I want you to cry uncle."

"Go ahead then. Punish me."

With a knee by each of Longarm's hip bones, she dropped back onto his erection, taking it still deeper. And then she began moving up and down with amazing vigor as she leaned forward, swinging her nipples across Longarm's face as she gasped frantically, "Take them!"

Reaching up with his mouth, he took one of her nipples and held it between his lips. She went wild then and began riding him harder and harder, lunging forward, then back, forward, then back—their bodies slapping together violently until Longarm found himself lunging up boldly to meet each of her thrusts. At last he could hold himself back no longer and, grabbing her hip bones, he began slamming her down onto him with a rough, rhythmic fury that had her gasping with pleasure.

This time when they both came in a series of bucking,

shuddering orgasms, Rosemary collapsed forward onto him. He caught her gently in his arms and placed her down beside him on the bed. She was barely conscious, but there was a smile on her face as she turned to look at him.

"I'm all filled up now, dear heart," she told him dreamily. "All filled up . . ."

"And I'm as empty as a rain barrel in August."

But she didn't hear. She was asleep this time, her face flushed, her eyes closed. Looking down at her, he thought she looked almost angelic—but the illusion lasted for only an instant.

He pulled the bedsheet up over her shoulder, closed his own eyes, and slept.

Chapter 3

The next day, late in the afternoon, Longarm left Rosemary at the hotel, crossed Harrison Avenue and walked to Winnie Purdy's parlor house on West Fifth Street, less than a block from the Clarendon. The door was answered by a petite black maid, who was forced to crane her neck to see up into his face. She was all giggles, bowed smartly at his request to see the mistress of the house, then left him standing in the parlor as she vanished in search of Winnie.

A moment later Winnie entered, all smiles, anxious to meet this first eager afternoon guest. Her girls, dressed scantily and fluttering like a flock of hens, followed in after her. Winnie, a large woman with more than ample cleavage and frizzy hair dyed an outrageous orange, was mildly disappointed that Longarm was not there on business—as were a few of the girls eyeing him from a long red leather sofa. The parlor and the adjoining rooms appeared to have been designed and decorated by a Moslem prince. Mirrors and scarlet tapestries covered the walls, and the rugs were thick enough to catch and hide a silver dollar.

Winnie escorted Longarm to the privacy of her tiny sitting room and listened attentively to his description of the missing duchess. When he had finished, she sighed and told him she could tell him nothing.

"She ain't the type my customers prefer, Marshal," she told him. "You might say I cater to a special type of men—them that likes their girls dark and full of hell—like Mexicans, Indians, and a few high yallers."

Longarm got to his feet. "Much obliged, Winnie. Think I'll have any trouble finding her if she's been working this town?"

"Not from your description of her. And if she's in the business, Marshal, she's working this town. For them as can keep themselves clean, there's more gold in my rooms upstairs than any miner will ever find underground."

Longarm smiled. "I can believe it."

Winnie got up also and, moving closer, winked up at him. "Sure you don't want to sample my latest girl, Marshal? She's fresh from the coast, part Spanish, part Indian. Clean as a sparrow an' as tight as a miser's purse."

"Thanks, but no thanks, Winnie."

As Longarm started from the place, Winnie hurried ahead of him, shooed the gawking professionals out of his way and escorted Longarm to the door. As she closed it behind him, Longarm heard a peal of laughter erupt from the girls.

Mopping his brow, Longarm squared his shoulders and crossed the street to Molly May's. Molly greeted him warmly, and as soon as she saw his badge and learned his business, she hauled him into the kitchen past her gaping girls and joined him in a beer at the kitchen table. Her hair was up in curlers and her nose was as round and red as a cherry. A cheerful woman, she listened carefully to his description of Jane-Marie, perking up considerably when she heard the girl was from England.

"A blonde, you say—and with lots of fire."

Longarm nodded.

"Try Frankie Paige's," she said emphatically, lifting her beer mug and downing its contents.

"You've seen this girl?"

Wiping her mouth with the back of her hand, she shook her head. "Nope. But I've heard of her. Seems she brought Frankie some grief a while back."

"What name's she using?"

"Sarah. Sarah Smith, if I'm not mistaken."

Longarm nodded. Jane-Marie was not showing much imagination when it came to inventing names. Sarah Jones in New Orleans, Sarah Smith in Leadville. He got to his feet.

"Thanks, Molly."

"Stay a while. We got time for another brew, ain't we, Custis?"

"You have, but I haven't. Thanks again."

Longarm clapped his hat onto his head and left by the kitchen door rather than wade through the fascinating gauntlet of painted women waiting in the parlor.

None of Frankie Paige's girls were in sight when, summoned by her servant girl, Frankie entered her parlor. Indeed, the large house was as hushed and quiet as a hospital. Frankie Paige herself was a tiny woman with jet black hair piled high atop her head in what was an obvious attempt to increase her height. But the cold, glittering light in her green eyes was enough in itself to intimidate any girl or guest. Her waist was as narrow as a wasp's, her movements brisk, almost masculine. She wore her rouge skillfully and in the dim light of her garish, mirror-walled parlor, she looked barely twenty herself. But in the clear light of her very businesslike office, she looked every single one of her forty years.

"Yes, Marshal," she said, moving around behind her desk and sitting down. "What can I do for you?"

"May I sit down?"

"Of course." She tried to smile, but the steel in her face would not entirely allow it.

Longarm sat and gave Frankie a description of Jane-Marie.

"Yes," Frankie snapped. "She was one of my girls."

"Was?"

"You heard me," Frankie told him, icy hatred gleaming in her hard eyes.

"I gather you were not fond of her."

"She was a hot little bitch who thought her shit didn't stink. It did."

"Do you have any idea where she could be now?" he asked.

"I do."

Longarm waited. Frankie leaned forward on her desk, her hard eyes fixing Longarm with a gaze that almost nailed him to his chair. "I want it understood," she told him coldly, "that if I help you find this high-born bitch, I will not be drawn into it any further. I am not responsible for her actions while she was in my employ—or afterwards."

"What actions?"

Frankie leaned back in her chair, her eyes narrowing. "Three weeks ago she robbed one of my best customers, Big Bill Barnstable, then ran off with Doc Hamlet. The next day Bill rode after them. They found his bones bleaching in the sun a week later."

"I see. And who might this Doc Hamlet be?"

"Runs a medicine show. Him and a black giant. Last I

30

heard they were heading for Blackwood."

"Could you describe his outfit for me?"

"Big flashy wagon. Used to be an army ambulance. It's got lots of red and gold trim. His team is four big black horses, as shiny black as the giant. I imagine this high-born lady is having a fine time servicing the black and the Doc."

"This Doc Hamlet—can you describe him?"

"As tall as you, a few years older, maybe. Gray hair, Vandyke beard. Best con man I ever saw, but he's met his match in this bitch you're after."

The almost palpable hatred Frankie felt for Jane-Marie seemed to fill the air of the room with its cold breath. Longarm stood up and put his hat back on.

"I guess you've told me enough, Frankie. As you say, you sure can't be held responsible for this girl's actions."

Frankie got to her feet. "I'll show you out," she said, leading him from her office.

As she pulled the outside door open for Longarm, he turned to her. "Much obliged for your time, Frankie," he told her.

"Just nail that bitch's ass to the wall for me, Marshal," she said, as Longarm stepped out past her.

Before Longarm could reply, Frankie shut the door behind him.

Rosemary was visibly upset. "But, Longarm, I simply can't believe it! Are you sure this woman Miss Paige described is really Jane-Marie?"

"She seemed pretty certain—and she had no reason to lie, Rosemary."

"But I *know* Jane-Marie. I grew up with her. She could never have done what that woman said!"

"Stranger things have happened, Rosemary."

They were in the hotel dining room. Longarm had held

off telling Rosemary what he had learned until she finished her meal. But once their coffee was in front of them, Longarm had related word for word Frankie Paige's account of Jane-Marie's brief employment at her place, her subsequent flight, and the death that followed.

"Well, I want to see this Miss Paige myself," Rosemary said. "I am sure she is mistaken."

"You can do that if you wish, Rosemary. But no matter how reliable or unreliable you may think Frankie Paige is, I'll be leaving for Blackwood first thing in the morning."

"Without me?"

"I think you'd be better off staying right here, Rosemary. One man is already dead, and this is beginning to sound a lot more grim than either Vail or I had bargained for."

"I'm not afraid."

"Well, maybe you should be. The point is, I don't think I'll be needing you to find Jane-Marie now. A medicine show with an oversized black and a beautiful woman with corn-silk hair should be enough of an attraction to alert the entire countryside. I'll have no trouble tracking her now."

"I don't care! I'm going with you."

"I wish you wouldn't."

"Longarm, I insist. I've come all this way. You can't leave me out of this now!"

He smiled wearily and finished his coffee. He had not really expected her to let him leave her behind in Leadville, but he had felt obliged to make the effort. "All right," he told her gently. "All right."

She beamed happily at him and sat back in her chair, relieved. Then she leaned toward him again. "But first I am going to see that madam. It won't hurt any for me to make positively certain it *was* Jane-Marie, will it?"

"Of course not. But I warn you, Frankie Paige is not a

pleasant woman. Finish your coffee. I'll wait for you on the hotel porch. And don't take too long. We'll need our sleep. The stage for Blackwood leaves at seven."

As Rosemary lifted the coffee to her lips, her eyes peered at him mischievously across the rim of her cup. "When I come back, do we have to go right to sleep, Longarm?"

He chuckled and shook his head. He had had no intention of doing anything of the kind.

The almost empty stage rattled and swayed as it neared the crest of the stage road. Looking out past the leather curtains, Longarm saw sheer cliffs rising out of sight, rugged, wiry conifers clinging to its face. On the other side, he knew, the drop was almost straight down.

A round, pink-faced whiskey drummer was sitting on the seat facing him. Beside the drummer sat a large Indian wearing a derby hat, checked vest, and ancient leggings. A huge bowie knife was stuck in the red sash he had wrapped around his ample waist. As he sat staring impassively ahead, his big moon face reminded Longarm of a wax cigar-store Indian melting in the sun.

Rosemary sat silently beside Longarm. Their lovemaking the night before had lost some of its exuberance, which he attributed to Rosemary's unsettling interview with Frankie Paige. It had evidently convinced Rosemary that the girl Frankie described to Longarm was indeed Jane-Marie. Recalling the madam's steely gaze and her fierce loathing of Jane-Marie, Longarm understood perfectly how dispirited Rosemary must now feel.

While waiting for the stage this morning, she had remained silent and troubled, even though she made gallant attempts at times to smile back at him or to lighten the conversation. Now, a full two hours out of Leadville, she had given in to her melancholy and lapsed into silence, gazing out past the leather curtains with unfocused, distant eyes.

Longarm finished his second cheroot, tossed it out the window, and leaned back in his seat, content to sit and gaze out the window. He expected they would reach Blackwood by nightfall, and as soon as they found a hotel, Longarm intended to begin his inquiries. This was, he realized glumly, becoming a somewhat dispiriting assignment—following after a woman who appeared to leave nothing but trouble—and now death, in her wake.

Longarm thrust away these gloomy reflections and tried to take some interest in the rough terrain over which the stage was moving. They had almost reached the crest of the stage road now. The team was laboring and the stage itself was barely moving.

Suddenly there came the sharp cry of the jehu, followed almost immediately by the bark of a handgun. As the jehu pulled his team to a scrambling halt, Longarm poked his head out of the window and saw four masked riders planted in front of the stage. In the lead rider's hand was a smoking sixgun. As Longarm watched, the shotgun messenger, still clasping his shotgun, tumbled lifeless to the ground.

The four riders moved swiftly to surround the stage. Longarm started to reach for his .44, then thought better of it. The hail of bullets that would follow such a move would only endanger the other passengers, Rosemary included.

One of the outlaws, obviously the ringleader, shouted up at the jehu to throw down the strongbox, then come down after it. It was flung down promptly, landing heavily on the ground before his mount. As the jehu clambered down and stood by helplessly, the highwayman immediately dismounted, shot off the lock, and began transferring the gold and Treasury notes to his saddlebags. Meanwhile, the other three members of his gang, their bandannas still masking

34

the lower portion of their faces, had dismounted and were approaching the stage with drawn guns.

One of them flung open the door and, poking his gun at the passengers, snarled, "Out of there, all of you — and don't make no sudden moves. This here gun's got a real hair trigger."

Longarm was the closest to the door. As he stepped out, the outlaw reached deftly over, pulled Longarm's Colt from his cross-draw rig, and flung it among the rocks alongside the road.

"Stand over there," he told Longarm. As the others climbed out, he bid them line up alongside Longarm.

Rosemary took her place coolly beside Longarm, her eyes watching the robbers with something close to fascination. The whiskey drummer was trembling as he held on to his sample case and the Indian stood stoically beside the drummer, his obsidian eyes regarding the three highwaymen with impassive contempt.

By this time the leader of the gang had finished looting the contents of the strongbox. As he approached the other three, a saddlebag draped over one shoulder, his eyes looked shrewdly over the passengers. He was a husky man, with unruly locks of jet-black hair sticking out from under the sweatband of his tan, floppy-brimmed hat. As he approached, he swaggered somewhat. He was a man evidently accustomed to robbing stages.

"This all there is?" he asked his men. "Just four passengers?"

"Looks like it," said one of his men, a shorter, squatter outlaw with a low forehead and nervous, beady eyes.

"Well, get what you can, then, Matt — and let's ride."

"What about the girl?" said another one. This outlaw was the youngest of the bunch, judging from the sound of his voice, and his eyes glittered as he looked over Rosemary.

35

"Take her, too, if you want."

Rosemary gasped and moved closer to Longarm.

"Never mind the girl," said Longarm. "Just take our valuables and be satisfied with that."

The leader laughed. "You think you're in charge here, do you, mister?"

Stepping closer, the outlaw called Matt swung his revolver and clubbed Longarm on the side of the head. Longarm went reeling back, tried to stay on his feet, then felt a second blow, this one crunching down onto the top of his head. His knees gave way and he heard Rosemary scream.

Flat on his back, Longarm looked up through painfully slitted eyes as the outlaw knelt close beside him. His bandanna had slipped down off his face. He was grinning. His teeth resembled a rotting picket fence and he smelled of rancid sweat and whiskey. Looking beyond the outlaw, Longarm saw Rosemary struggling with the younger highwayman, while the whiskey drummer hastily emptied his purse and wallet into the leader's saddlebag. Behind the drummer, the big Indian was slowly backing up as another of the four highwaymen approached him with drawn gun.

Bending close to Longarm, Matt reached into the lawman's side pocket and pulled out his wallet. When he opened it and saw the silver federal badge pinned to its inside, he got quickly to his feet.

"Looky what we got here!" he cried, flashing the badge at the leader.

The gang leader nodded curtly, almost as if he had been expecting this. "Kill him," he said.

Rosemary screamed. "No!" she cried. "Don't! Please!"

Ignoring her cry, Matt turned back to Longarm, cocked his Colt, and aimed carefully down at Longarm. By this time, Longarm had managed to slip the derringer from his vest pocket and cock it. He squeezed off two quick shots.

The outlaw seemed more startled than hurt as the two .44 slugs stamped dark holes in his vest, each slug raising a small plume of dust. Then, without a word, the outlaw dropped his gun and pitched forward to the ground. He landed as heavily as a sack of potatoes and did not move again.

Pandemonium broke loose. With a blood-curdling war cry, the big Indian suddenly rushed the outlaw who had been advancing on him. In the scuffle that followed, the outlaw's gun detonated. The Indian was hit. Yet this only seemed to arouse the Indian to still greater fury. He flung himself upon the outlaw and bore him to the ground. Lifting his bowie over his head, he brought the flashing blade down again and again with swift, metronomic efficiency.

Meanwhile, the whiskey drummer and the jehu were racing for cover among the rocks. The gang leader turned and fired a wild shot after them. Then he spun about to deal with Longarm who, at that moment, was in the act of reaching for the revolver of the outlaw he had just killed.

"Hold it right there, you son of a bitch!" the man cried, uncocking his Colt and leveling it on Longarm.

A distant rifle shot sent a round into the ground at the outlaw's feet. He jumped back, startled. Immediately a second shot echoed high above them among the rocks. This time the round ricocheted off the face of a boulder only inches from the outlaw's head.

With a cry to the outlaw holding Rosemary, the highwaymen holstered his weapon, leaped astride his mount, and wheeled about. Flinging the screaming, kicking Rosemary across his pommel, the other one followed after him. Longarm picked up the dead outlaw's Colt but held his fire for fear of hitting Rosemary.

Holstering the weapon, he got to his feet and started to run toward one of the fallen outlaws' mounts. But his legs turned to rubber, and he found himself reeling forward into a red mist. A curtain of blood was flowing down over his eyes from the scalp laceration. Reaching out blindly for the horse's reins, he missed and sagged stupidly to the ground.

Pushing himself to a sitting position, he looked up and saw the big Indian looming over him.

"You stay quiet," the Indian said. "You have flat head now for while."

Then the Indian sat cross-legged before Longarm and peered mournfully into his face. He reminded Longarm of a Saint Bernard dog.

Nodding wearily, Longarm waited patiently for the hammering in his head to stop. When it subsided somewhat, he took out his handkerchief and wiped off his forehead and his eyes. He did not dare touch the top of his head. It felt as if an army of Chinese coolies were blasting a railroad tunnel through it.

The Indian's drooping face leaned closer as he regarded Longarm intently. He had recovered his derby hat.

"I will call you Blood in the Eyes," he said.

"And what are you called?"

"Once Tall Buffalo it was. But now must I think it be Old Buffalo."

The outlaw's slug had hit the Indian high in the meaty portion of his right shoulder. A dark patch of blood extended from the wound, down across his checkered vest all the way to his red sash. As the Indian stood over Longarm, he held his left arm against his bare chest, his fingers resting inside his vest. But aside from this careful cradling of his right arm, the Indian appeared to be experiencing little difficulty.

The clink of iron shoes on stone came clearly to them both. They turned to see a lone rider approaching. He held a Winchester across the pommel of his saddle and, as he rode closer, he peered at them anxiously. Behind him, stealing cautiously out from behind the rocks, came the jehu and the whiskey drummer.

The rider was wearing a tan, high-crowned plainsman's hat. It was so fresh and clean it might have just been taken from the box. A linen duster was worn over a tan duck coat and brown twill pants, which were stuffed neatly into a newly purchased pair of finely tooled riding boots. The rifle, a gleaming Winchester, appeared just as new.

As the rider pulled to a halt before the two of them and dismounted, Longarm got to his feet to greet him. The stranger was dressed like a greenhorn. But, judging from the way he had just handled that new rifle of his, that didn't matter.

Not one bit.

Chapter 4

Longarm stuck out his hand. "Name's Long, Custis Long," he told the stranger. "My friends call me Longarm. Right pleased to meet you."

Seen closer, the fellow had a thin, meticulously trimmed mustache, a thin beak of a nose, and a jaw that was square and solid. His large, expressive mouth widened suddenly into a warm smile.

"I'm Alfred Bolt. Pleased to meet you, Custis." Then he looked around him at the two dead outlaws sprawled in the dust. "I was some distance when I heard the first shots. I rode as fast as I could. But it seems to me you and this here aborigine have done pretty well for yourselves."

"But not well enough," Longarm remarked bleakly. "They got away with the money and the girl."

Old Buffalo stepped closer to Bolt, his mournful eyes peering intently at the man. "Not am I what you say. I am Old Buffalo."

"I assure you Old Buffalo," Bolt replied hastily, "I meant no disrespect. Of what tribe are you?"

"My people, they are the Sioux," Old Buffalo said, straightening carefully. His shoulder wound was quite obviously giving him some trouble now.

"It is a pleasure to meet you," Bolt said. He peered more closely at Old Buffalo's wound. "I think we should see to that wound of yours immediately, Old Buffalo," he told him with a concerned frown. "I have surgical dressings and instruments in my bedroll."

"It is nothing," the Indian said, holding himself still more erect. "About such flea bites Old Buffalo, worry he does not."

Surprised, Bolt laughed. Shrugging, he turned back to Longarm. "And what about you, Longarm? Your scalp appeared to be rather cruelly plowed up."

"I'll live," said Longarm, reaching carefully down and picking up his hat. "By the way, that was good shooting back there. Thanks."

"I would have preferred a rifle with a longer range," Bolt replied. "Nevertheless, this Winchester is an excellent firearm."

"You sound like a stranger to these parts," Longarm noted.

Bolt answered carefully, "My dear sir, except for the aborigines, isn't every white man a stranger in this wild West of yours?"

Longarm shrugged. "I guess maybe you could say that."

Old Buffalo nodded solemnly. "That is true. White man is stranger to red man's land. He not listen to voice of wind! He not read sign. He pay no heed to voice of red man. So rip it up our land he does with plow, and with long gun, kills he all the buffalo!"

Astonished at this speech, Longarm and Bolt were at a

loss as to how to reply when the jehu and the whiskey drummer pulled up beside them. Both men were breathing hard. During the past few minutes, they had done a considerable amount of running in both directions.

"We got to bring this stage on into Blackwood, mister," the jehu told Longarm, hastily mopping his florid, perspiring face. He was short, powerfully built fellow with large gnarled hands. "Them robbers done kilt old Tom Hickman."

"He was the shotgun messenger?" Longarm asked.

The jehu nodded vigorously. "And he just signed on to the job last month."

"You got any idea who that was leading those outlaws?"

"Sure. Jim Blade. I recognized his voice right off. That was Jim Blade, and the one what took the girl was his kid brother, Tommy. Them two's been hounding this country hereabouts for close on to a year now."

"You go on to Blackwood," Longarm told him. "I'm going to take one of these mounts they've left behind and go after them."

"In that case," Bolt told Longarm, "you may count on my assistance."

"Come too will Old Buffalo," said the Indian.

"Thanks," Longarm told them both. "Much obliged."

"All right then. Suit yourself," said the jehu, turning and hurrying toward the dead shotgun messenger. "But right now I'll need help with Tom's body."

After Longarm and Bolt had finished lifting the dead shotgun messenger into the coach's rear boot, the jehu inspected his team, then clambered up into his box and handed down to Longarm his rifle and carpetbag. As the whiskey drummer clambered hastily into the stage, the jehu nodded a curt goodbye to them and reached for his whip.

"I say, driver!" Bolt called up to him. "What about these two dead outlaws? Aren't you going to take them in, also?"

"What fer?"

"Why, to bury them, of course!"

The jehu spat a large gob of tobacco juice at the nearest corpse. "Hell's fire! Let the sons of bitches rot in the sun. The buzzards'll take care of them soon enough."

Bolt looked up at the sky, his blue eyes narrowing, and caught sight of three buzzards already drifting lazily in the hot, still air. "Yes," he said musingly, "I suppose you are right."

The jehu swung back around in his seat and sent his whip cracking out over the backs of his team. As the stage lurched forward and disappeared in a sudden rooster tail of gravel and thick dust, Longarm went searching for his .44 among the rocks where the outlaw had thrown it. He found the revolver, inspected it closely, and was pleased to find it was still in good working order.

He dropped it into his cross-draw rig, then walked over to Old Buffalo. Handing him the outlaw's gun, Longarm asked, "Think maybe you could use this?"

The gleam in the Indian's eyes was his answer. He took the gun and thrust it into his red sash. Then he bent over the dead outlaw and stripped the cartridge-laden gunbelt from him. Looping the belt over his right shoulder, he smiled at Longarm.

"Now Indian you see will help track outlaw good!"

Longarm nodded and headed for the outlaw horse he had chosen, a big black. He was pleased. An Indian could track a rattlesnake across a waxed floor.

A day later, still on the outlaws' trail, the three men pulled up about noon on the crest of a pine-topped ridge and gazed down the slope at the torturous, canyon-slashed badlands stretching as far as the horizon. So far Old Buffalo's keen eyes, despite his wound, had been able to keep them on the

44

outlaw's trail. But now the big, moon-faced Indian was beginning to show signs of wearying.

Dismounting, Longarm pulled his mount out of the blistering sun and in under some pines. He didn't know what he could do about Old Buffalo's wounds, but he had an idea, from what Bolt had said earlier, that Bolt might be able to do something.

One thing was for sure: Old Buffalo needed it.

Once they had tended to their mounts and settled in under the trees, Bolt coaxed the big Indian to the ground and had him rest back against a tree. Then he lifted aside the checked vest and examined the wound. Looking over Bolt's shoulder, Longarm could see that it was festering. An ugly zone of red, inflamed flesh completely surrounded the entry wound.

"That bullet will have to come out," said Bolt, turning and glancing up at Longarm.

Longarm nodded. "Think you can do it?"

Bolt got to his feet. "I'll get my bag," he said. "I'd appreciate it if you would start a fire. I'll need it to cauterize the wound and sterilize my instruments."

"You a doctor, Bolt?"

"No, I am not."

Without another word, Bolt went for his instruments and Longarm started to look for firewood.

A moment later Bolt pulled out of his black bag a bottle of laudanum, a scalpel, and a bullet probe shaped like an elongated pair of scissors with small wire loops on the end of each blade. Longarm had never seen such a curious-looking bullet probe before.

Catching the surprise on Longarm's face, Bolt said, "I've carried this probe with me since I served in India. The medical officer of my brigade fashioned them. During an emergency in the field, I assisted him in surgery. When he died later of cholera, he gave me this medical bag and his instruments. I have found this probe of his a considerable improvement over most others."

The campfire was going briskly by this time. After filling a coffeepot with water from his canteen and setting it in the fire, Bolt handed the scalpel and the probe to Longarm and instructed him to hold them in the fire.

Then he turned his attention to Old Buffalo, peeling the Indian's checked vest back over his head. For a moment or two he peered unhappily at the wound, then glanced at Longarm.

"I think I'll be needing your help in holding our patient down while I probe for the bullet," he said.

Old Buffalo immediately responded. "Longarm not hold down Old Buffalo," the Indian insisted, his obsidian eyes gleaming angrily. "No squaw Old Buffalo is. Of pain not he afraid!"

Bolt gazed at the Indian for a moment, then shrugged. "In that case, I'll proceed."

Bolt took a clean shirt from his bedroll, tore it into strips, and poured the boiling water from the coffeepot onto them. Then he carefully folded the steaming strips on a flat rock close by and turned his attention to the Indian.

"Lie back," Bolt told him.

As meekly as a child, the Indian did as he was told. Bolt bent over the Indian's huge barrel of a chest.

Glancing quickly back at Longarm, Bolt said, "I'd like the scalpel, please."

Longarm pulled it out of the fire and handed it, handle first, to him. Swiftly, deftly, Bolt lanced the area around the entry wound. As the skin puckered back, an unpleasant ooze of black blood and pus poured forth. Again Bolt's scalpel flashed and still more festering ooze leaked out. After swabbing out the area with the still-steaming cloths, Bolt

46

handed back the scalpel and asked Longarm for the probe.

Grasping it firmly, he plunged it deep into the wound. It raised steam, and the smell of searing flesh filled Longarm's nostrils. He glanced at the Indian. Old Buffalo remained perfectly still as he gazed past them up at the sky, apparently lost in contemplation of the shifting clouds.

Bolt was having trouble. Cursing slightly, he bent still closer and sent the probe in still deeper. Longarm glanced at Old Buffalo. The big Indian's chest trembled slightly, and in that instant Longarm realized that Old Buffalo was not lost in any dream at all—that he was feeling everything.

"Ah!" Bolt cried softly.

Pulling out the probe, he held up the mashed, bloodsoaked bullet for Old Buffalo to see. The Indian nodded slightly, then let his head fall back onto the ground and promptly passed out.

Bolt spent another ten minutes or so swabbing out the wound with the scalding swabs of cloth. Then he tore a second of his shirts into strips to provide bandages. A few moments later, when Old Buffalo regained consciousness, he found himself propped up against the tree, his upper torso completely encircled by a tight bandage, his right arm in a sling.

He looked about him in some wonderment. "Dreams come to Old Buffalo," he said. "Wake up I do not want. Dreams come. The buffalo again I see and like the wind I ride. Once more Tall Buffalo I am."

Bolt smiled. "Fine. Sleep now. You need it, I think. And perhaps the dreams will come again."

The Indian regarded Bolt for a long moment. Then, nodding slightly, he closed his eyes and was instantly asleep.

Bolt got to his feet and gazed down at the big Indian. After a moment he smiled, then glanced at Longarm. "He's

47

as tough as they come. I think he'll make it."

"If you're not a doctor, Bolt," Longarm told him, "maybe you should be."

"Perhaps. It was what I wanted," he admitted, as he closed up his black bag. "Unfortunately, I was born with a silver spoon in my mouth. Such a worthy profession was deemed beneath a man of my station."

"You say you served in India."

Bolt got to his feet and started to walk over to his horse. "Yes," he said, "with the Bengal Lancers."

"Guess maybe that's where you learned to ride and fire a rifle," Longarm commented as he walked with the man over to his horse.

"That, and a few other things not nearly as useful," Bolt admitted, as he opened up his bedroll and packed away the black bag.

When he finished tying his bedroll down, Longarm handed him a cheroot. "Join me in a smoke," Longarm said. "After all that, I need something to calm my stomach down."

Bolt grinned. "Me, too," he said, taking the cheroot gratefully.

As the two men found a shady spot and made themselves comfortable, Bolt lit up the cheroot, took a few puffs, then turned to Longarm and asked about the girl they were trying to liberate from Jim Blade and his brother.

When Longarm finished his description of Rosemary, Bolt remained silent for a long while. Then, staring intently at the glowing tip of his cheroot, he asked, "Do you trust this woman?"

Longarm was somewhat surprised at the question, but he considered a moment before replying. Then, with a short laugh, he said, "Of course not."

Bolt grinned and nodded. "Good," he said.

And that ended the discussion.

• • •

The next day Old Buffalo insisted he was ready to ride, and indeed he had little difficulty picking up the outlaws' sign as they descended into the badlands.

But by the middle of the afternoon, the clouds, which had been sitting on the horizon in great, massed formations, began to move toward them. They swirled and collided, merging and building, while flickering tongues of lightning lit the dark vaults of their interiors. Dim, distant mutterings became occasional crashes as the clouds swept toward them over the badlands, piling higher and higher in tumbling mountains, growing ever upward, their great anvil heads flattening out.

The wind was rising. Sand stung their faces. Longarm pulled his bandanna up over his mouth and nostrils. The air was crackling now with dry heat, and Longarm could smell the ozone. No rain was falling yet, but forks of lightning were bombarding the buttes and pinnacles ahead of them.

Halfway down the western sky remained clear, shining in under the rapidly closing ceiling of dense clouds. But not for long, as the line of black, tumbling clouds cracked and split with a roar like that of cannonballs tumbling down a marble stairway. Then the sun went out.

Longarm pulled up. Old Buffalo and Bolt did likewise. Longarm looked back down the narrow arroyo they were following. It was dry now, but it wouldn't be for long. Even as he thought this, a large drop of rain splattered noisily on the dust of the trail.

Old Buffalo turned his horse and looked back at Longarm. He was thinking the same thing. "Better soon we get out of here," he said.

Longarm nodded. "And quick."

They were halfway up the side of the canyon, their horses' hooves scrambling frantically on the loose shale, when the first heavy drops of rain began to fall, thumping on their backs and on the rims of their hats with loud, angry slaps. Just as they reached the canyon rim, there was a sound like cloth tearing. A bolt of lightning rent the air, and the clouds opened up above them.

Like heavy water poured from buckets, the rain came down, each drop hitting like buckshot. Longarm's arms and back were lashed unmercifully, plastering his shirt and coat to his body, drumming on his hat like hailstones, running off his brim in a miniature waterfall. On all sides the air was rent with snapping, shuddering clasps of thunder, while the air danced with the continuous flickering sheets of lightning. The smell of brimstone filled Longarm's nostrils.

They found shelter of a sort under a rocky overhang close by the canyon's rim. Dismounting, they huddled together miserably. At last—after about thirty minutes, and as suddenly as it had begun—the storm passed. The muttering clouds swept on past them, the pounding rain became a shower and then a drizzle. Longarm saw Old Buffalo walk out from under the overhang and peer down into the arroyo they had just left. He appeared to be waiting for something.

As soon as the rain had let up completely, Longarm and Bolt walked over to the Indian and peered with him down into the canyon they had just left. They saw only standing water and a few small waterfalls as the runoff tumbled down off the rim. But before long, they heard as well as felt a queer vibration under their feet, like a freight train thundering down a steep grade. A moment later a wall of water surged around a bend in the arroyo. Red as tomato soup, thick as gravy, and heavy with mud and sand, lathered with scuds of brown froth, the flash flood roared through the narrow gorge, sweeping up and carrying all before it—shrubs, small trees, and boulders.

Had they stayed down there during the cloudburst, they

would have been caught up in that fearsome cataract's path and been sucked to oblivion. As it was, all trace of the outlaws' trail they had been following was gone now, swept away with everything else.

Longarm hated to admit it to himself, but by now Blade and his brother had long since reached their hideout somewhere deep in the badland's intricate maze of rock and mesa. And without a trail to follow, an army of trackers would not be able to find it.

It was too bad, but as Bolt had reminded him, he did not entirely trust Rosemary—and he still had a lost duchess to find.

Turning from the canyon rim, he walked back to his black and mounted up. As he did so, he looked back at Old Buffalo and Bolt.

"Looks like we got no more trail to follow," he told them. "I'm headin' on in to Blackwood. I got some unfinished business waiting for me there. You two gents are welcome to join me."

Bolt shrugged. "We've come this far," he said, reaching for his horse's reins.

Old Buffalo said nothing. He just swung into his saddle and looked impassively at Longarm. Pleased, Longarm swung his back around and led the way due west toward Blackwood.

Chapter 5

A little after nightfall, they reached Blackwood. Sheer, towering rock faces enclosed the town on both sides, and through its center trailed a narrow, miserable stream. Crowded close upon it were a motley of tents, raw, unpainted hotels, gambling saloons, and whorehouses. As the three men clopped loudly across the plank bridge leading into the town, Longarm caught sight of a milling, torch-lit crowd farther down the street.

The three riders kept on past the empty saloons and deserted gambling halls until they reached the crowd demonstrating angrily in front of a small, flimsily constructed jailhouse. Next to it a fresh gallows had apparently just been erected, its raw wood gleaming in the torches' lurid light. The night air was filled with shouts and curses. As the three riders pulled up, they heard a leather-lunged miner, his speech punctuated by roars of assent, urging immediate and final action.

Longarm dismounted and dropped his reins over a hitch rail. As Bolt and the Indian dismounted also, Longarm commented, "Looks like we're just in time for a necktie party."

Bolt nodded grimly.

Old Buffalo shifted his feet. "Bad way is hanging to die. White man, him no civilized, I think."

Longarm stared at the Indian. "Well now, Old Buffalo, I've seen how the civilized Sioux finish off their enemies."

Old Buffalo smiled sheepishly. "Longarm right. I hear Quaker agent say that. Maybe Sioux not civilized too."

Turning back to the crowd, Longarm caught sight of the jehu and waved to him. The coach driver saw them and waved back, then left the crowd and hurried across the street to them.

"You gents finally got here, did you?" he asked. "Any luck rescuin' that pretty lady?"

"Nope."

"Didn't think you would. This here's rugged country. No one's been able to nail Jim Blade's gang yet. He knows this mountain country like the palm of his hand."

"Looks like you've got some excitement," said Bolt.

The jehu nodded eagerly, his eyes lighting up. "There's goin' to be a necktie party tonight—instead of tomorrow."

"Why the hurry?"

"The town marshal took sick after he tried Doc Hamlet's medicine, and died about an hour ago. That there Doc Hamlet's been selling poison!"

"Doc Hamlet, you say?" asked Longarm.

"That's the one. Him and that black giant of his. They been selling their medicine outside town for the past week. Only it ain't been curin' anybody, and now it's done kilt the marshal."

54

"You sure it was the Doc's medicine killed him?"

The jehu nodded vigorously. "Ain't no question. Widow Parker took sick as soon as she tried it, and so did Cal Timmons and a passel of others. The Doc tole ever'body it was used by the crowned heads of Europe. Hell, if that's true, I figure them kings should all be dead by now."

"You got a sample?" Longarm asked.

From his back pocket, the jehu produced a small black bottle and handed it to Longarm. Longarm quickly read the label:

DR. NELSON T. HAMLET'S GOLDEN MEDICAL DISCOVERY
The Great Indian Medicine!
Is a compound of the virtues of Roots, Herbs,
Barks, Gums, and Leaves. Its elements are Blood-
making, Blood-cleansing and Life-sustaining.
It is the Purest, Safest, and Most Effectual
Cathartic Medicine known to the Public.
The science of Medicine and Chemistry have never
produced so valuable a remedy, nor one so potent
to cure all diseases arising from an impure blood.
WILL CURE
Constipation,   Liver Complaint,   Dyspepsia,
Indigestion, Loss of Appetite, Scrofula,
Rheumatism, Chills and Fever,
or Any Disease
(arising from an impure blood or Deranged Liver)
PRICE $1.00 PER BOTTLE

Longarm shook his head at the potion's far-fetched claims, unstoppered the bottle, and lowered his nose carefully to it. It smelled potent enough—a combination of licorice and alcohol, for the most part—but God only knew what other combination of ingredients Doc Hamlet had packed into his miracle cure. Longarm stoppered the bottle and handed it back to the jehu.

"You been taking any of this?" he inquired of the jehu.

"I been using it to clean out the inside of the stagecoach. It sure as hell kills fleas and ticks."

Bolt laughed.

"Where's the ambulance the Doc was using—and the girl who was traveling with him?"

The jehu smiled. "You mean that blonde?"

"That's who I mean."

"She lit out with the ambulance when trouble started."

"Leaving Doc Hamlet behind?"

"That's right. But we figure he was planning on meeting her somewhere else. Him and his black partner was saddlin' up when the rest of us overhauled them."

"How long before the hanging, do you figure?"

The jehu looked back at the mob. A miner was up on the jail porch making a speech while the crowd cheered him on. He looked and sounded very drunk. But that didn't seem to matter.

"Won't be long now," the jehu assured Longarm. "I figure the deputy's just about got the message by now."

Longarm glanced away from the jehu at the jailhouse. He could see a shadowy figure standing in the single window. That would be the deputy. He looked back at the jehu.

"Who's the deputy?"

"Young feller. Pete Adams—full of bullshit about law and order."

"You mean there hasn't been a trial yet?"

"Nope. And we don't expect the circuit judge for another couple of weeks."

"This'll be a lynching, then."

"Hell! Them two deserve it. The town marshal didn't

die pretty. And the Widow Parker's in a real bad way. So Pete better stand aside or he'll get trampled in the rush. This here crowd means business."

Looking over the shouting, milling mob, Longarm nodded. They sure as hell did mean business, that much was obvious. Which meant Longarm had to do something and do it quick if he wanted to get from the Doc some lead on Jane-Marie's possible whereabouts. Maybe they had planned to meet somewhere later.

Longarm dismissed the jehu with a curt nod, then turned to glance into the saloon they'd tied up in front of.

"Let's go in here, gents," he suggested to Bolt and Old Buffalo. "I crave something to wet my tonsils. We've been swallowing dust long enough."

Bolt and the Indian followed Longarm up the saloon's porch steps. The barkeep, a sawed-off shotgun in his hand, was standing just behind the batwings, watching the torch-lit crowd with glittering eyes. Like all the others, it seemed, he too was eager to watch a hanging.

A heavy, lethargic man with a pale face and a bulbous nose, he stepped back as the three men pushed through the batwings, then reluctantly left his post by the door and moved around behind the bar as they bellied up to it.

"Rye," Longarm said hopefully. "Maryland."

"We got whiskey and beer. I don't know where the hell any of it comes from. Which do you want?"

"Whiskey," Longarm told him, spinning a coin onto the bar.

The barkeep lifted a whiskey bottle onto the mahogany and placed two shot glasses down in front of them. "We don't serve redskins in this here establishment," he told Longarm. "It's against the law."

Longarm reached across the bar and grabbed the barkeep's shirt, then pulled him halfway up onto the bar, his

57

.44 materializing in his right hand. He cocked the revolver and rested its muzzle gently on the barkeep's large nose.

"I'll have another shot glass and no more shit from you," Longarm told him quietly, "or there'll be a killin' before there'll be a hangin'."

His eyes bugging out of his head, the barkeep nodded desperately. Longarm released him. The fellow promptly slapped a third shot glass down onto the bar.

"Now let's have that shotgun."

As the fellow lifted it up over the bar, Longarm cautioned him sharply. The barkeep carefully turned the Greener so that its stock was facing toward Longarm. Longarm holstered his own weapon, took the shotgun, and gave it to Bolt to carry. Then he took up the bottle and his shot glass and led his two companions across the bar to a table along the wall.

Slumping into a chair, he took the shotgun back from Old Buffalo and laid it across the table in full sight of the barkeep. Then he looked coldly across the saloon at him. "Go on back over to the door," Longarm told him, "and let me know if that deputy brings out them two prisoners."

The barkeep hustled out from behind the bar. Longarm poured for Bolt and Old Buffalo. As the Indian lifted the shot glass to his lips, Longarm cocked an eyebrow at him. "You better show me it ain't true all Indians can't hold their liquor."

The heavy folds in Old Buffalo's face lifted in a smile. "See you will. Indian when he want, hold his liquor. He not want most time. He like drunk. But not this time, maybe."

"That's right. Not this time."

The three men drank up. Longarm wiped his mouth, then leaned forward and spoke softly to Bolt and Old Buffalo. "I need the help of those two in that jail. It looks like we'll have to get them out of there. You two with me?"

Bolt and Old Buffalo nodded. Then the Indian held up one finger. "One more shot first."

Longarm poured.

Bolt pushed his glass forward also and Longarm filled it. "You mind telling us what this is all about?" Bolt asked. "How come you're so anxious to spring those two? From what I gather, they rather deserve the rope."

"I agree, Bolt," Longarm said, filling his own glass. "They deserve to be hung for selling that poisonous concoction to innocent dupes. But there's been no due process as far as I can see—and, as a deputy U. S. marshal, I'm sworn to stop lynchings. It ain't legal."

"And that girl you asked the stage driver about—this blonde—what is her part in all this?"

"She's the one I'm out here to find and bring safely back to Denver."

Bolt's eyebrows canted upward slightly. He studied Longarm with new interest. "Would you care to tell me any more about her?"

"Only to tell you that she's not wanted for any wrong-doin'—not yet, anyway."

"A lost sheep, is it? A runaway?"

"You could put it that way," Longarm replied, sipping his whiskey. "By the way, Bolt, I don't suppose you'd be willin' to tell me what you're doing out here in the middle of nowhere all decked out in a fancy duster and a new rifle? You're English ... and so's that woman I'm after. There wouldn't be any connection, would there?"

Bolt finished his drink and got to his feet. "The truth of the matter is, I'm not at liberty to say," he said, smiling amiably down at Longarm. "But you have my word, sir. When the time seems more propitious, I'll be more than happy to enlighten you fully."

Longarm shrugged. "Fair enough."

"Now, just how do you suggest we go about rescuing those two snake-oil salesmen from the justified ire of that crowd out there?"

"Never saw a mob that wasn't a coward at heart. We'll face them down. Call their bluff." Longarm looked at Old Buffalo. "Slip out the back of this saloon and find the livery. We'll need two more good horses. When we leave this town, I'm thinking we'll have an angry bunch of riders at our back."

"You want me steal horses?" Old Buffalo's eyes gleamed.

"No. Tell the owner of the livery stable I'm a federal marshal and I'll settle up with him later."

Old Buffalo seemed mildly disappointed at this as he finished his drink and got to his feet. A moment later the big Indian had melted into the darkness at the rear of the saloon and vanished out the back. Picking up the shotgun he had rescued from the barkeep, Longarm got up and started for the door, Bolt following.

The barkeep turned as they approached. From the look on his face, it was clear his anger at Longarm's earlier treatment of him had not abated.

"Step out of the way and keep your ass down," Longarm advised him.

The barkeep slouched to one side.

Longarm stepped out onto the porch. An alley ran beside the saloon and emptied onto the crowded street. Longarm looked at Bolt. "You cover me from the other side of that alley," he said. "Don't shoot unless you have to."

"What are you going to do?"

"I told you—face the bastards down."

Longarm watched as Bolt stepped down off the saloon porch and lifted his Winchester from its scabbard, then hurried across the alley. Taking a position in a darkened doorway, Bolt took out his sixgun, then leaned his Winchester against the door beside him. As soon as he was ready, Longarm took out his .44 and sent a shot into the air. Its sudden, thunderous detonation startled the crowd. Every face swiveled about to look up at him standing on the porch.

Longarm cupped his left hand around his mouth and shouted, "Deputy!"

The jailhouse door swung open and the deputy stood in the doorway, his figure dark against the bright lantern light behind him. "Who's that?" he called. "Who fired that shot?"

"I did," Longarm responded. "Deputy U. S. Marshal Long." Longarm looked over the crowd. "Step aside," he told those men closest. "I'm comin' through."

He stepped down from the porch and strode toward the crowd. Those in the first rank who were not quick enough to get out of his way found themselves shouldered roughly aside. Reluctantly, the rest of the crowd parted for him. A moment later he was mounting the steps in front of the jailhouse.

The deputy was young, all right, probably not more than eighteen years of age, but already a tall, gangling individual with wide shoulders and a steady, purposeful gleam in his eyes. He too was carrying a shotgun.

"You must be crazy, Marshal," the deputy said uneasily. "This here crowd is out for blood."

"You want to hand the prisoners over to this mob?"

"I do not."

"Then I suggest you back my play," Longarm told him.

"Suits me, Marshal. I'd just about used up all my options."

Longarm turned about, the shotgun resting in the crook of his right arm. He said nothing for a minute or two, content to look over the crowd, to fix a few of the miners with his eyes, then shift his gaze. He cleared his throat.

61

"All right, you bravos," he told them, the sarcasm and scorn enough to scorch those closest. "I'm going to say this only once. I am not alone. I have other men with me. And one of them is standing over there in the shadow of that doorway." Longarm pointed. "Like me, he's well armed and not afraid to use his weapon."

The miners turned in a body to look at Bolt. As soon as they did so, Bolt stepped boldly toward them so they could see him more clearly. The crowd swung its attention back to Longarm.

"Go on back to your gaming tables," Longarm told them, "or your girls. Drink up. Forget these two in here. There'll be no lynching tonight."

"So you say!" someone shouted.

"There's a hundred of us. You may get one or two, but we'll get those two bastards in there!" someone else shouted.

"All right. Fine," Longarm told them. He smiled grimly. "So which one of you will it be first?"

There was an uneasy stirring in the front ranks. A few men looked nervously at their neighbors and started to inch back. Longarm stepped down off the porch and approached one fellow. He looked big enough to hunt bears with a switch. Immediately the fellow started to push back against the miner behind him.

"You going to be first, mister?"

"Hell, no!" the fellow shouted as he turned hastily and clawed his way back through the crowd.

Longarm swung to face another one. If he was not mistaken, this fellow had been one of those shouting the loudest earlier. A tall, gaunt man with wild, feverish eyes, he flinched when he saw Longarm lift the shotgun and aim it at him.

"How about you?" Longarm asked.

"Hell, no!" the man cried.

Others in the back jeered then, but the gaunt man paid no attention. He pushed frantically back against those behind him, his right arm held up over his face to protect himself.

"All right!" Longarm cried, turning to face the others. "Who is it going to be? Who wants to lose his life just to hang those two no-accounts in there?"

The crowd milled unhappily, sullenly. At the rear a few turned and started to slip off down the street. Others followed. Longarm watched the crowd a moment longer, then turned his back on it and mounted the jailhouse steps.

As he was turning back around to face the crowd, a shot rang out from a tight group of men on his far right. The deputy staggered back through the doorway. Another shot came from a second grop just in front of the jail. Longarm heard the slug slam into the doorjamb and slipped the safety off his shotgun. Bolt broke into the crowd from the rear, heading for the tight knot of men from which the second shot had come.

The crowd broke in all directions. Racing through its remnants, Bolt fired at one fellow who was bringing up his smoking Colt. Bolt's slug hit the miner, pitching him forward to the ground.

Longarm saw another miner. He too had a smoking gun in hand and was racing down the street. This was the one who had hit the deputy. But before Longarm could bring him down, Old Buffalo, astride his own mount and leading the two other horses he had gone for, galloped straight for him. The miner veered to one side and tried to bring up his weapon. Before he could, the Indian reached down and caught him about his shirt collar. Yanking him off the ground, Old Buffalo dragged him a ways toward the jailhouse, then flung him aside. Weaponless, on all fours, the miner scrambled for cover.

Old Buffalo pulled his mount to a scrambling halt in front of the jailhouse, dismounted, and joined Longarm and Bolt on the porch.

"Stay here and guard the horses," Longarm told him. "We'll be leavin' this town fast."

Then he and Bolt hurried into the jail. The deputy, clutching his right bicep, was sitting up in his chair, his face ashen.

"How do you feel?" Longarm asked him.

"I'll live."

Longarm peered at the shoulder wound. The bullet had gone right through. It was painful but not a fatal wound. "Just a flesh wound," Longarm told him. "Where's the keys?"

With a nod the deputy indicated a pile of keys on his desk.

Longarm snatched them up and hurried into the cellblock. Unlocking the cell door, he pulled it open and led the two prisoners out. Doc Hamlet was just as Frankie Paige had described him—as tall as Longarm, with thick gray hair and a well-trimmed Vandyke beard. His assistant, a giant of a black, seemed considerably shaken. Indeed, both men were close to panic as Longarm pushed them ahead of him into the town marshal's office.

"You two are in luck," the deputy told them. "This federal marshal is takin' you out of here."

"You mean you ain't goin' to hang us?" the Doc asked, astonished.

"That ain't because we admire you all that much," Longarm told him. "It happens to be against the law to hang anyone without a trial. There's horses waitin' outside. Let's go!"

Without further explanation, Longarm and Bolt pushed the two prisoners ahead of them out the door. As the two hurried off the porch to mount the horses Old Buffalo was holding for them, Longarm and Bolt dashed across the street to their own mounts. Cracking open the shotgun and dumping out the shells, Longarm flung the empty Greener through the saloon's batwings and mounted up.

"Move out!" he called across the street to Old Buffalo.

The big Indian wheeled his mount and charged back through Blackwood at full gallop. The two prisoners rode clumsily but managed to keep up, Longarm and Bolt close behind. They were only a few yards from the plank bridge when gunfire erupted in their rear and lead began whining over their heads.

Longarm heard Bolt curse savagely, but said nothing himself as he leaned low over his horse's neck and spurred him toward the bridge.

They were not out of the woods yet.

Chapter 6

The miners were persistent. Not until late the next day could Longarm be sure they had shaken their pursuers.

With their mounts just about ready to give out, they pulled up on a low ridge. There was a stream close by, and the pines on the ridge would offer some shelter. Longarm called a halt. They'd found their camp for the night.

A few minutes later, as Longarm off-saddled his horse, he noticed how stiffly Doc Hamlet and his black companion—by now Longarm knew him as Will Clay—got off their mounts and saw to them. The two men were not used to riding horseback, it seemed—at least not at the pace they had been forced to maintain since the night before.

Dropping his saddle and the rest of his gear under a pine, Longarm glanced over at Old Buffalo. "What did you tell the stable owner about these horses?"

Old Buffalo looked mournfully at Longarm. "Owner not there. Only stove-up cowboy see me. In stall hide he. Tell him I we some day bring back horses—and not burn down his town or his woman steal. He happy then. To me he show many horse."

Longarm considered a moment, then shrugged. There was nothing he could do about it now. He would straighten it all out when he got back to Denver. Vail would think of something. He'd have to. It wouldn't do for word to get out that Vail's operatives were going around stealing horses, no matter what the need.

Longarm had not had much chance to talk to Hamlet. It was clear the man was astonished at his deliverance and somewhat reluctant to discuss the third member of his party, the absent Sarah Smith. After watering his mount and then hobbling it, Longarm approached Hamlet. The fellow was standing alone by the stream, a perplexed and troubled look on his face. Some distance away, Will Clay was hunkered down nervously under a cottonwood.

"Guess maybe you're wondering why we went to all this trouble for you two," Longarm commented coldly, taking out a cheroot and lighting it. He did not offer one to Hamlet.

"Frankly, yes."

"It's Sarah Smith I'm interested in. You left Leadville with her, so I was hopin' you'd be able to help me find her—or at least give me some clue as to her whereabouts."

"I told you, Marshal. She just ran out on me. She's a devil, that one. I am sure it was she who poisoned that crate of elixir."

"You mean Dr. Hamlet's Golden Medical Discovery?"

"You may laugh, sir! But that medicine has remarkable powers. Will and I have taken it every day for the past year, and it has breathed new life into both of us!"

"No more impure blood, eh?"

"Precisely. Any ill health brought on by impure blood or deranged livers is immediately cured by this famous elixir.

And now that bitch has ruined me. She has taken my entire supply, my ambulance, and my horses, and run off!"

"You must have some idea which way she went."

Hamlet looked long and hard at Longarm. "You are right," he said finally. "I do."

"Well?"

"Would you mind telling me why you are so interested in this woman?"

"That is none of your business."

"You're a lawman. It is natural for me to conclude your interest in her is official. Is she wanted for any . . . trouble? Bad trouble?"

"Like murder?"

The man's eyes lit up. "Then you do know about that? You're trackin' her for the murder of Big Bill!"

"You're ranging pretty far ahead of me, Doc. All I know for sure is Barnstable's body was found some time after you and Sarah Smith left Leadville. The way I figure it, you're in just about as much trouble concerning that business as Sarah Smith is. Now, you got something you want to tell me?"

Doc Hamlet swallowed. He looked for a moment as if he were about to say something—but only for a moment. "No," he said. "I was just wondering, is all."

"You sure of that?"

"I'm sure."

"I think you're a liar. But right now I'm asking you to tell me which way you figure Sarah Smith went."

"To Digger Falls."

Longarm had heard about Digger Falls. It was really booming. Some said it was close to becoming another Virginia City. Both gold and silver had been discovered in the mountains nearby. So far it looked like a real bonanza. It was another two days' ride, at least, straight through the pass they had been approaching all that morning.

"What makes you think she'd head for Digger Falls?"

"Because that's where I was planning to go next."

"And she knows how to get there?"

"Sure. She was the one who usually drove the team. She's getting to know this country pretty well."

"And you say she poisoned your elixir."

"Every last bottle."

"You're willing to swear to that, are you?"

"I am."

"So you're telling me Sarah Smith is on her way to Digger Falls to poison the miners."

"More than likely," Doc Hamlet insisted, but not nearly as stoutly as before. "Hell, Marshal, I know that woman. And there's no telling *what* she'll do next."

"Thanks for your help, Doc," Longarm drawled.

He left the Doc then and started for the pines. Bolt and Old Buffalo had already started a campfire and were fixing supper. Longarm could smell the coffee.

Longarm was puzzled and more than a little curious. He was chasing after a woman who, if he found her in time, would become a member of British high society. It was not inconceivable that some day she might become a confidante to the Queen. Yet so far she had managed to employ herself with unmistakable enthusiasm in some of the most famous and not-so-famous cathouses in the West. In addition, she was involved in the murder of one man, and—if Hamlet's accusation was correct—she was also guilty of killing by poison a local town marshal.

Longarm shook his head as he wondered what new deviltry this lost duchess would have committed by the time he finally did catch up to her—and, when he did, if he should dare to bring her back to Denver to become the new Duchess of Clyde.

Longarm awoke suddenly, aware of movement in the night. He sat up. Old Buffalo was hurrying through the pines toward him, Bolt at his side. Longarm threw aside the flap of his soogan and got to his feet.

"What is it?"

"Them two we free from jail," Old Buffalo told him. "Horses they take, and go." He raised an arm and pointed.

Longarm looked in the direction Old Buffalo pointed and saw the two fleeing riders, bathed for a moment in a sudden splash of moonlight, disappearing over a low ridge. They were heading south, away from the pass. He swore. He had wanted to dig a little deeper into Big Bill Barnstable's killing.

Then he sighed and shrugged. "Let them go," he said to the two men. "They'll hang themselves sooner or later. Good riddance. Now let's get some sleep. We'll get an early start in the morning."

They were approaching the pass when Old Buffalo pulled up and pointed to some wagon tracks in a stretch of sand.

"Ambulance wagon. That Doc feller tell truth."

Bolt seemed pleased. "She's come this way, all right."

They came upon undeniable evidence not long after. Cresting a slight ridge, they saw one side of the trail littered with packing crates. Surrounding the crates were shattered bottles of Doc Hamlet's Golden Medical Discovery. His elixir had oozed out of the broken bottles and now covered the ground with a black, noisome carpet that stained the rocks and seemed to have soaked deep into the ground.

The result was a dead place. The bunch grass and saplings and any other vegetation caught within its dark reach had wilted and died. An air of lifelessness hung over the small patch of ground. It was as if Doc Hamlet's famed compound of roots, herbs, barks, gums, and leaves had turned this patch of ground beside the trail into a place of desolation and death.

"Jesus," said Bolt, "what in hell was *in* that stuff, anyway?"

"The safest, purest, and most effective cathartic known," Longarm drawled ironically, repeating the inscription on the bottles.

"You think Doc Hamlet was telling the truth about this here Sarah Smith putting poison in this elixir?" Bolt asked.

Longarm looked at him. It was obvious the man's question was not a casual one.

"I don't know for sure," Longarm replied. "But I don't see how she could have put poison in every bottle. It would have taken some doing. And, from the smell of that stuff, I don't think she had to do much of anything to make that so-called medicine lethal. I figure whatever that fool Doc put in these bottles in the first place finally went rancid—or maybe just started to cook."

Bolt looked back at the dark patch of desolation and nodded. "Yes," he said. "I agree."

Longarm kneed his mount forward. "Let's get the hell away from this stench," he said. "I'm beginning to feel a mite queasy myself."

Old Buffalo nodded. "Sick I am too already," he said. "Ride ahead now I will."

He clapped his heels to his horse and led the way on toward the pass.

Grinning, Longarm watched him go, then gave his horse his rein and followed after him. Bolt wasted no time either.

They got through the pass a little before nightfall and caught sight of a small ranch off to the right under a small clutch of cottonwood. Longarm was glad to see it. There was a well in front, which meant fresh water. The horse barn looked large enough to handle all three of their mounts, and if they were lucky enough the rancher's wife would more than likely have a goodly supply of fresh coffee, if nothing else.

They turned off the trail and rode the quarter of a mile or so to the ranch. As they rode into the small compound, a gaunt woman, her dress torn, her hair in wild disarray, appeared in the ranch-house doorway.

"The cholera!" she cried. "We got it. Stay back!"

At once the three riders pulled to a halt. Old Buffalo looked uneasily at Longarm and Bolt. Behind the woman, her husband appeared, then three young ones, a girl and two boys. The oldest, a flaxen-haired girl, could not have been more than ten. The five of them presented a mournful, cadaverous appearance; the children especially were little more than gaunt scarecrows.

Longarm introduced himself and his two companions. The man told them he was Sam Perkins, and introduced Longarm and his companions to his wife and the rest of his family. Their youngest, Perkins explained, was still in bed. He had been the sickest.

"How long have you had the cholera?" Bolt asked.

"More'n a week," said Perkins.

Bolt glanced at Longarm. "I've dealt with cholera before, in India. If this family is up and about now, it looks like they'll pull through."

"But I wouldn't trust the water," Longarm replied.

"Hell, no. They should most certainly boil it before using it. Ideally, they should haul out all their bedding and burn that as well, and get rid of any food they still have in the house."

73

"We can't do that, mister," said Perkins. "This here bed-din' is all we got. And we got little enough food as it is."

Bolt shrugged. "Well, all I can say is you're lucky to be alive."

"Well, we wouldn't have made it," said Perkins's wife, "if it warn't for that lady come by."

"What lady?" Longarm asked.

"The woman drivin' that purty ambulance," she replied. "She came right in when we was the sickest. We told her it was the cholera, but she didn't pay us no mind. She nursed us all. Kept feeding us and covering us up against the chills. She boiled the water and all our bedding and our clothes. We was a mess, all five of us, but I never saw a body work so hard to keep us and the place clean."

"A real angel of mercy was what she was," said Perkins.

"A blonde girl, was she?" Longarm asked.

"Yes," said the woman quickly. "And she had the nicest accent."

"When did she leave?" Longarm asked.

"About three days ago. And before she left, she made us promise we'd boil the water from now on."

"Did anyone in your family die?" Bolt asked.

"Little Andy almost did," the mother responded. "He was the worst. But Miss Sarah, she nursed him like he was her own."

Bolt looked at Longarm. "From the description, that's Sarah Smith, all right. That means we're not that far behind her now. I think I'd better stay here and help these people. They're still pretty weak, and they just might get careless. You go on into Digger Falls. I'll catch up later."

"You sure you want to do this?" Longarm asked.

"Like I said, I've dealt with cholera before. I'll be all right."

Old Buffalo spoke up then. "I stay with Bolt. But I make

camp there," he said, pointing to a ridge overlooking the cabin. "There from white man's sickness I will be safe."

Longarm shrugged. "Suit yourself."

"Thanks, Old Buffalo," said Bolt. "I welcome your company."

Longarm bid the family, then Bolt and Old Buffalo goodbye, after which he turned his mount and rode back out of the compound. When he looked back a moment later, Bolt had already dismounted and was walking toward the cabin, while Old Buffalo was lifting dust on his way to the ridge. Longarm turned back around and urged his mount on.

He wished them both luck, but he was glad he was not going into that cabin.

It was an hour or so before sundown when Longarm caught the quick glint of sunlight on a rifle barrel high in the rocks ahead of him.

Twice during the last couple of hours he had glimpsed the momentary outline of horsemen on the rimrocks high above the trail, some distance behind him. That he was being followed he had no doubt. This was the first time, however, that he had caught any sign ahead of him. It was clear that if he were to hold to the course he was now following, when he reached the rocks he might come under deadly fire.

He turned his horse off the trail. Keeping a heavy stand of timber between him and the high rocks ahead, he rode directly toward the spot where he had caught sight of the waiting rifleman. When he reached the timber a moment later, he rode right into it.

Dusk was falling when he tethered his mount to a sapling at the edge of the timber. He snaked his Winchester out of its scabbard and moved into the rocks at the base of the

75

escarpment. A minute before, peering up at the rim, he had seen the dark outline of a horseman. Now, as he clambered up the steep slope, he expected to hear at any moment the echoing crack of a rifle.

He moved from boulder to boulder, clinging momentarily to shaky outcroppings and ledges. Not a single shot broke the uncanny stillness. When at last he reached the crest of the escarpment, emerging out of the slope's deep shadow to the wan light of a fading sunset, he caught sight of fresh hoofprints on the ground before him.

Glancing about warily, he ducked swiftly across the cap-rock to a line of stunted timber just ahead of him. Reaching it, he levered a fresh cartridge into the rifle's firing chamber, then crouched low and waited.

He did not have to wait long.

From his left a horseman emerged from a clump of cottonwood and moved slowly along the ridge, his rifle resting across the pommel of his saddle. Every now and then he paused to peer intently down at the trail far below. He was almost directly across from Longarm when two other horsemen—one of whom Longarm recognized as the younger Blade—cantered onto the flat from the other direction and rode up to him.

When the three riders met, it was young Blade who spoke. He seemed to be insisting that someone would soon be showing up on the trail below them, while the fellow patrolling the rim was certain that whoever they had seen on the trail below had long since dismounted and made camp in the timber.

Letting them argue it out among themselves, Longarm slipped back into the timber, then cut through it toward the spot from which the two horsemen had just emerged. The sun had fallen below the horizon by this time, plunging the high plateau into a murky twilight, and he soon caught the glow of a campfire directly ahead of him.

Crouching low, his big frame slipping through the undergrowth as silently as a cat, he reached the outer perimeter of the campsite and crouched behind a clump of juniper. Parting its branches with the barrel of his rifle, he peered at the low fire and the two figures hunkered down before it.

One was the elder Blade. He was sipping a cup of coffee. Alongside him, his companion was smoking a cigarette and staring moodily into the flames. Neither man was talking. Longarm looked around for sign of Rosemary. He was about to conclude she was not with them when she emerged from the darkness on the far side of the campfire carrying a fresh load of firewood.

Longarm waited until she got close to the fire. Then he got to his feet and stepped out from behind the juniper, slipping off the safety catch on his Winchester. The sound it made was loud enough to alert the three.

"Longarm!" cried Rosemary, dropping the wood.

Jim Blade looked up in astonishment. His companion jumped to his feet, his hand dropping to his sixgun. Longarm pointed the rifle's muzzle at the man's gut.

"Go ahead," Longarm said softly. "Give me an excuse."

The outlaw froze. Slowly, carefully, Jim Blade got to his feet. "Damn you," he grated harshly, "where in hell did you come from?"

"Never mind that," Longarm said. "Just stand easy and unbuckle your gunbelts and let them drop." He glanced at Rosemary. "Get their guns."

As soon as they dropped their gunbelts, Rosemary gathered them up. Longarm took the weapons from her and flung them into the brush. Then he asked her where their horses were tethered. She pointed to some rocks about twenty yards distant.

"They keep them in a small grassy spot behind those rocks over there."

Longarm nodded. "All right," he told Blade and his companion, "pick up your saddles and carry them over to them rocks."

Reluctantly, the two men lugged their saddles through the gathering darkness. Once they reached the clearing on the other side of the rocks, Longarm stepped close behind both men and clubbed them to the ground. They were unconscious before they hit. After checking to make certain they were both breathing, Longarm selected two mounts and saddled up.

A moment later, Longarm and Rosemary rode off into the night.

Chapter 7

Close to midnight, they halted to make camp. Longarm had doubled back earlier to retrieve his own mount and gear, after which he had set loose the horse he had taken from Jim Blade. This had taken him longer than he had anticipated. By Longarm's reckoning, they were within twenty miles of Digger Falls, but their horses were just about ready to give out. And so was Rosemary, Longarm figured. That he had not collared Jim Blade and the rest of his gang bothered him. But at the same time he realized that if he had tried to bring them all in, he might have endangered Rosemary.

They made camp in a patch of timber above the trail they had been following, and with only one soogan between them, Longarm decided to offer it to Rosemary while he slept some distance away on some pine boughs.

"My," Rosemary said, after Longarm made the suggestion and dropped the soogan at her feet, "aren't you being gallant tonight!" The sharpness in her voice alerted Long-arm.

"What's the matter?" he asked. "Don't you want to sleep in the soogan?"

"Of course I do. But not under these conditions!"

Longarm frowned at her, exasperated. "Now, what in tarnation do you mean by that?"

"You know full well what I mean. You don't want me any more. You think I've been soiled!"

"Damn it, Rosemary, that's not it at all. We're tired. Both of us. We need to get us some shuteye!"

"Speak for yourself," she snapped angrily. "I don't remember complaining about being tired. That's the first time I heard *you* mention being tired. It's just an excuse, and you know it!"

Wearily, Longarm said, "Look, Rosemary. I really am tired. Sleep in the soogan or on the ground—or in a tree, if it makes you feel any better. It don't matter to me which."

"You see!" she wailed. "You admit it!"

With a helpless shrug, Longarm turned and walked over to the spot he had selected earlier and began gathering pine boughs. While he worked, he glanced up occasionally and in the moon's pale glow saw Rosemary fixing up the soogan. Her movements were quick and angry, and every once in a while she would glance furiously in his direction.

Women, he thought in some exasperation. *You never in hell can tell what one is thinking. Or what one is likely to do next.*

He pulled off his boots and tried to make himself comfortable on the pine boughs. When he figured he had managed it, he took off his hat and placed his Colt under his saddle, which he was using as a pillow. There was a cool breeze coming off the mountain peaks west of them. He pulled his slicker up over his shoulder and was drifting off when he became aware of Rosemary standing over him.

He opened one eye but didn't say anything, in hopes she would think him asleep and go back to her soogan. Instead, she flung the soogan down alongside him and knelt on it, her face hovering inches from his own.

"I will not be scorned!" she hissed. "And I never saw a man *that* tired."

She ducked her head forward, then yanked her nightgown over her head. As it spilled forward onto the soogan, she moved still closer to Longarm, her full, melon-like breasts glowing in the moonlight, her fingers reaching out for his fly. As she began unbuttoning it, Longarm opened both eyes and looked at Rosemary.

"I suppose you been saving up for this?"

"I most certainly have! I knew you'd come after me—and I didn't let one of those outlaws near me."

"You mean you had a choice?"

"No, but they did. I would cook for them and take care of them—but only if they let me be." She smiled. "And I let Jim Blade think he was the only one I favored."

"Clever. Very clever."

"So, you see, I was not soiled. And that means I am still yours to do with as you will."

Longarm didn't believe a word of it. But if he were going to get any sleep, he would simply have to accept Rosemary's offer. He had long since learned that the only thing worse than taking a woman against her will was *not* taking her when that was what she wanted.

In a moment she had pulled off his pants, then his longjohns. He shucked out of his shirt and undershirt and, with a sigh, joined her inside the soogan, fitting his long, naked body against hers. Rosemary's warmth aroused him at once.

She was right. No man was ever *that* tired.

81

As her hand reached down to encircle his engorged member, her lips found his, her tongue probing with wanton skill. After a long, distracting kiss, he pulled away from her and closed his lips about one of her nipples, his tongue flicking at it wickedly, transforming it into a small, up-thrusting bullet.

Inflamed, they began crawling over each other like wanton night creatures, their lips serving as eyes as they explored each other's hidden crevices and valleys and peaks. As her lips closed finally about his swelling manhood, his own nipped at her musky pubis, until both of them could hold off no longer.

Longarm pulled Rosemary in under him. Her legs splayed quickly, and as she lifted them high, he plunged home. She grunted as he struck bottom.

"You all right?" he asked.

"Don't talk!" she cried. "Oh, I've waited so long for you to find me again, Longarm! Go deeper! Deeper! I want *all* of you!"

Reaching up with one arm, she looped it around his neck, holding onto him fiercely as she began to gyrate wildly under him.

Though Longarm was dimly aware he should maybe slow down and take it a little easy, he found himself unable to do anything of the sort. He had not really been all that tired after all. He was like a wild man as he pounded away, while Rosemary answered each thrust of his with one of her own, pleading with him to go still deeper, to drive still harder.

Then, in a series of plunging spasms, Longarm came— implanting his seed deeper with each involuntary thrust. With a tiny, keening cry, Rosemary held fast to him, shuddering herself violently as she too came, thrusting hungrily upward, sucking him still deeper into her. At last, uttering a deep sigh, she fell back.

Still thoroughly aroused, Longarm dropped beside her, then kissed her on the lips, hard—and let his hand close about her warm, soaking pubis.

"Again?" she whispered.

For answer, his tongue reached deep into her mouth. At once she reached up and he felt her hand on the back of his head, pulling him still closer.

"Oh, my," she cried softly, as her hand dropped down to his crotch and found his still throbbing member. "You see? You weren't all that tired, now were you?"

"Guess not," he muttered, his voice sounding strange to his ears.

"Now!" she told him excitedly, pushing his back. "Let me!"

She eased up onto him, took one of her breasts and placed it near his mouth. He closed his lips about her nipple, hard. She groaned with pleasure, then scooted down, her hand reaching down for his erection. Her legs astride his narrow waist, she guided him past her lips, then lowered herself back onto his soaring erection.

"Ummm!" she murmured, sitting back and shaking out her dark penumbra of chestnut hair.

Longarm leaned back and let her close tightly about his erection. In the dim light, he thought he saw her smiling down from a great height.

"I love to ride horseback," she told Longarm huskily. "Bareback. Not sidesaddle."

"Like now?"

"Yes," she grunted. "Like now." Then, gasping, she worked herself down still further onto him. "Ohh," she moaned, "you're so damned big!"

"Shut up," he told her, "and get moving."

Leaning forward, she reached out and grabbed his shoulders and hung over him, her hair enveloping him in a fragrant tent, her alabaster breasts swinging close over his face, her nipples brushing his lips.

"Suck me," she cried. "Please, Longarm! Suck me!"

He lifted his head and took one of her nipples in his mouth and began to thrust upward at the same time. At once she began to rock back and forth, the tempo increasing until both of them were thrusting in wild unison, he lifting her high over him, she plunging down with a reckless, mindless urgency. Tiny, inarticulate cries broke from her lips. He reached out with both hands, grabbed her hip bones firmly, and proceeded to slam her down still more powerfully onto him.

At last they came, and it was like an eruption of molten lava as he felt himself spilling out of her and down across his thighs. In that instant, uttering the same keening cry she had loosed a moment before, Rosemary came a second time . . . and a third . . . and a fourth. . . .

At last, totally spent, Rosemary collapsed forward, hugging Longarm so closely her breasts nearly smothered him. Then she rolled off and they lay side by side in each other's arms. He could feel the tiny beads of perspiration that covered her body, and in the moon's pale sheen, her face seemed to glisten.

"Oh, my," Rosemary sighed. "You were certainly worth waiting for. Tell me, Longarm, did you miss me as much as I missed you?"

"Of course."

"You're just saying that, but I don't mind. I don't mind anything now. Ohh, you're so *good!*"

"You ain't so bad yourself," he responded.

"Let's sleep together in the soogan," she murmured drowsily.

He just nodded, too exhausted to argue—or pull himself out of the sleeping bag.

Her face resting on his chest, he closed his eyes and finally slept.

As Rosemary made coffee the next morning, Longarm told her what he had found out so far about Jane-Marie. When he had finished, Rosemary handed him a cup of coffee and shook her head emphatically.

"I don't think for one minute that Jane-Marie poisoned that medicine. I agree with you. The medicine just went bad."

Longarm sipped the hot coffee and nodded. "The same woman who risked her life to nurse that family wouldn't have slipped poison into those bottles of medicine."

Rosemary smiled. "They called her an angel of mercy. Wait until Jane-Marie hears that."

"But we still have to deal with that charge of Frankie Paige's," Longarm reminded her.

"What charge?"

"That she was responsible for the murder of Big Bill Barnstable."

She frowned. "Yes. How terrible! Do you really think she had a hand in that?"

Longarm shrugged. "When I see Jane-Marie, I guess that will be one of the first questions I will have to ask her. I'm hoping she will have an explanation."

"I am sure she will, Longarm."

Longarm finished his coffee and handed the cup back to Rosemary. Not long after, the two were astride their mounts, heading for Digger Falls.

They reached the booming mining town late that same afternoon.

Typical of most boom towns, Digger Falls was an unplanned motley of tents, unpainted frame shacks, and imposing two- and three-story buildings. Men in top hats and frock coats shared the wooden sidewalks with pallid, sleek-looking gamblers, confidence men, miners, and roustabouts in stocking caps and checkered shirts. Escorted women, attired modestly in long skirts and bonnets, found themselves jostled by gaudy, unescorted whores, whose long, unpinned, uncovered curls fell clear to their shoulders, and whose skirts were hiked high enough to reveal fetching ankles.

On all sides came the sound of hammers and saws as the town continued its building boom. A large saloon and gambling hall was nearing completion on one corner, and across from it an ornate opera house was celebrating its grand opening, with Artemus Ward that night's featured attraction. And, despite the early hour, every saloon and gaming house was running wide open.

As Longarm and Rosemary rode down Main Street, they had a difficult time avoiding the huge, high-sided ore wagons lumbering past them to the stamp mills on the slopes high above the town, their constant booming echoing and reechoing with metronomic regularity throughout the town and the enclosing hills.

Sighting a livery stable opposite the New International Hotel, Longarm and Rosemary rode up to it. Dismounting, they led their mounts into the stable and gave them to the hostler. Longarm unsaddled his mount and took his rifle and bedroll with him as he and Rosemary crossed the street to the hotel.

He registered for both of them, choosing separate rooms, despite Rosemary's impish protest that such an added expense was really not necessary.

"Dear heart," Rosemary whispered, as they followed the ancient bellhop up the stairs, "were you afraid you'd succumb to my charms?"

86

"Just careful," he told her, grinning wryly. "We got business in this town, remember. Jane-Marie may be here somewhere and we've come a long way to find her."

"I haven't forgotten at all," Rosemary responded, laughing. "But I'm sure Mr. Vail would appreciate it if we could cut some of our expenses. I was just thinking of him, that's all."

"Of course you were," Longarm said, pushing open his door. "I'm going across to the barbershop to get freshened up. See you downstairs in about an hour."

"All right," Rosemary called. "Until then."

After a steaming hot bath in the back of the barber shop, Longarm treated himself to a shave and a haircut, then purchased a fresh pack of cheroots. He was seated on the hotel veranda, puffing on one of them and watching the motley crowd flowing past the hotel, when Rosemary appeared.

"I need clothes," she told him, approaching his chair. "I had no idea how destitute I looked until I glanced into my dresser mirror."

Longarm sighed, reached into his pocket, and pulled out his wallet. Handing her some bills, he said, "You're right. I should have thought of that. I imagine your suitcase and things are still waiting for you in the Blackwood stage office."

"Is there any way we can get them?"

"While you're shopping I'll go down to the express office and see if they can send them along."

"I'd appreciate it, Longarm."

He watched her hurry off, then got to his feet and started down the veranda steps.

The express office was only a block away. He explained to the clerk what he wanted, and the fellow assured Longarm that Rosemary's things would be sent along promptly. Longarm thanked the man and left the office. On his way back to the hotel, however, he found himself pausing in front of a large, very busy saloon. The piano player was a good one and the sound of poker chips wafted out through the busy batwings. Longarm was about to enter when he caught a glimpse of a gaudily painted ambulance cutting down a side street, four handsome black horses in the traces. A black boy, obviously a servant, was driving it.

Longarm spun and pushed his way back through the crowd until he reached the corner. Glancing down the narrow street, all he could see at first were buggies and hansom cabs and oversized ore carriers. Then he glimpsed the sleek backsides of the four strutting horses as they turned another corner. He hurried after the ambulance as fast as the crowded sidewalk would allow, but by the time he reached his second corner, the wagon was nowhere in sight.

He glanced up at the street sign. Magnolia Street. Then he looked back down the street again and at once recognized it for what it was—the town's tenderloin. Small, two-story parlor houses, their curtains drawn and all of them neatly painted, lined both sides of the street.

He decided he would return to this street with Rosemary first thing in the morning. It would be foolish to attempt to find Jane-Marie now. The girls and madams would all be quite busy this time of night.

Three days later, neither Longarm nor Rosemary had been able to locate Jane-Marie. But on the fourth day, Longarm glimpsed the ambulance again, this time issuing from an alley that ran behind Magnolia Street. Dragging Rosemary hastily after him, he managed to overtake the ambulance as it waited to move into the next intersection.

If it were not for the horses, Longarm would not have

recognized it. No longer did the ambulance resemble a circus wagon. It had been painted a shining black. The only dash of color was the wheels' red spokes. The black boy driving it was outfitted now in a stunning red livery, shiny black boots, and a black visored cap.

"Hold up there, boy!" Longarm called, stepping out from the sidewalk.

The young black was just turning onto the next street. He yanked back on the reins and looked with some surprise down at Longarm.

"What do you want, mister? Ah ain't done nothin'."

"No, you haven't, and that's the truth," Longarm told him. "I'd just like a word with you."

"Ah can't hold up here, mister. There's other wagons behind me."

Longarm stepped up onto the seat beside the boy, then turned and held out his hand to Rosemary. Taking her hand, he hauled her up beside him on the seat.

"Move on," he told the boy. "I'll explain later." At the same time he dropped a silver coin into his hand.

The boy grinned and pocketed the coin, "Oh, Ah see," he said. "You couldn't get a ride downtown. Where do you and your lady friend want to go, mister?"

"The New International Hotel."

"Sure. Ah go right by there. You just hang on."

Longarm leaned back. Then, after a few minutes, he said, "This is a real fancy rig."

"Yes, sir. It belongs to my mistress," the boy said proudly.

"Looks brand new. Did she just get it?"

The boy nodded vigorously. "Only had it a week now. It sure comes in handy. Now all her customers can get a free ride to her place. And at night they don't have to walk back through all the mud and duck them ore carriers. Sure was a fine idea."

89

Longarm smiled at the boy. "And of course the men all tip, don't they?"

"Most of them," the boy nodded eagerly, "especially when Ah takes them back late at night."

Longarm looked at Rosemary. Pay dirt. A madam had most likely purchased the rig from Jane-Marie and was putting it to good use indeed—probably on Jane-Marie's advice.

"What's your mistress's name?" Longarm asked.

"Madam Julie," he said.

"On Magnolia Street?"

"No, sir," he said, glancing nervously at Rosemary. He obviously felt a little shy giving directions to a cathouse with a respectable lady within earshot. "It's two streets over. Horner Street."

"And what number would that be?"

Again the boy glanced unhappily at Rosemary. "Forty-two, sir."

By this time they had arrived at the hotel. As the boy pulled up, Longarm dropped another coin into his palm, then jumped down to the street and helped Rosemary to the ground. He tipped his hat to the young driver, who broke into a pleased grin and drove off.

"We've found her. I'm sure of it," said Rosemary. "Let's go there right now. It's early enough so they won't be busy."

"Do you think you'd better let me go? After all . . ."

"Longarm, don't be silly. I'm not a child."

"No, you certainly are not a child. But what's your hurry?"

"Have you any idea how long it has been since I've seen Jane-Marie? How anxious I am to see her after all she's been through?"

He nodded quickly. Of course. He shouldn't have wondered. It would have been strange if Rosemary were not this anxious.

90

"Okay, then. Let's go."

Number Forty-two Horner Street was a large, three-story house that fairly gleamed from a fresh coat of paint that must have been applied less than a week before. All the curtains were an appropriate scarlet, and when Longarm yanked the bell, its chime from deep within the house was pleasantly melodious.

A tall Indian girl answered the door. Longarm doffed his cap. "I'd like to see Madam Julie," he told her.

"And who shall I say is calling?" the servant girl inquired politely in impeccable English. "We do not open until eight-thirty this evening."

For answer, Longarm took out his wallet and showed the girl his badge. "Just tell the madam I am Deputy U. S. Marshal Custis Long."

The girl showed no emotion, just nodded slightly and stepped back, pulling the door open for them. "If you will please step inside," she told him, "I will fetch Madam Julie."

Longarm and Rosemary entered the small entrance hall. Scarlet curtains were fitted to the inner doorway leading from it. Their feet sank noiselessly into the thick rug. The maid closed the door behind them, flitted past them, and disappeared into the parlor beyond. A moment later a strikingly tall woman with dark red hair and keen hazel eyes glided toward them, a quizzical frown on her face.

"Melody tells me you have a badge," she said to Longarm, as if she had been delighted at the news. "Whatever made you think you would need that to get in?" Her voice went cold then and her eyes became icicles. "I am always willing to cooperate with the authorities—especially since my girls service so many of them for so very little."

Then she saw Rosemary, who was standing half hidden by the scarlet drapes.

Julie frowned at Rosemary, then glanced back at Longarm. "Tell me, Marshal. What is it you—and your friend—want?"

At once Longarm introduced Rosemary. Then after the formalities, Longarm asked the madam about the ambulance she had just purchased for her customers. "Would you mind telling me who you purchased it from?" he asked.

"Why? Is it stolen?"

"Not really."

Julie decided she would have to unbend a little. "Would you care to come inside—you, Miss Sutcliff?"

"That's very kind of you," said Longarm.

When all three were comfortably seated in the living room, the girl reappeared, and before Longarm could protest, Madam Julie ordered tea. As the servant vanished, the madam turned back to Longarm and fixed him with a cold stare.

"Would you care to be a little more exact, Deputy Long? Is the ambulance stolen property or is it not?"

"I can't be any more exact than I have been. Let's just say the gent that once owned it is no longer accountable."

The servant girl returned with a tray containing a solid silver tea service with cups and saucers of the finest bone china, all of which, Longarm realized, must have set Madam Julie back quite a bit. They remained silent while the maid poured their tea and handed a cup to each of them, along with a small pastry.

"I think I understand," Madam Julie said, when the girl had finished serving them. "The previous owner of this ambulance is wanted for some crime or other."

"There is a girl involved," Longarm began. "We are interested in finding her."

"You mean Sarah?" Madam Julie asked, in some surprise.

"Yes."

"Why? She's not in any trouble, is she?"

"If we could just see her," Rosemary said anxiously.

With a shrug, Madam Julie got to her feet and walked to an inner sitting room. Longarm heard the tinkle of soft feminine laughter, followed by the light patter of footsteps as someone hurried up carpeted stairs. Madam Julie reappeared, sat back down, and picked up her cup of tea, a puzzled frown on her face.

A few moments later the girl Longarm and Rosemary had so long been seeking paused in the living room doorway. Longarm was not impressed. Jane-Marie's lack of vitality disappointed him. She was a blonde, all right, but her eyes were faded and washed out, her manner slack, even slovenly. And then Longarm forced himself to remember what this poor girl had been through these past months—and chided himself for his ungenerous thoughts.

As Jane-Marie entered the room, Rosemary gasped, her hand clutching Longarm's arm. He turned quickly to her. "What's wrong?"

"Longarm, we've been following the wrong woman!"

"What's that?"

"This girl *isn't* Jane-Marie!"

Chapter 8

"Of course I'm not Jane-Marie!" the blonde girl replied, staring in some surprise at Rosemary. "I'm Sarah Farnsworth."

"Sarah who?" Longarm demanded.

"I told you. Farnsworth."

Belatedly remembering his manners, Longarm excused his bluntness and introduced himself and Rosemary. Then he said to her, "Now, would you mind telling me where you got that ambulance?"

Madam Julie got quickly to her feet and moved around the chair to stand beside the girl. "I believe I can answer that, Marshal. Sarah purchased the ambulance for me. It was for sale. I saw the advertisement in the newspaper. It was just what I wanted, so I gave Sarah the money and sent her after it."

Longarm turned to the girl. "Then you bought the ambulance from somebody in town here?"

"Yes."

"Who?"

"A woman."

"Do you know her name?"

"Sarah Smith."

Rosemary gasped and got to her feet.

"Where was she staying?" Longarm asked.

Sarah Farnsworth laughed. It was a cruel, mocking laugh. "At the livery stable."

"The livery?" Rosemary gasped.

"Yes. She was in rags and penniless. That's why she sold the wagon. She needed the money for food and clothing."

"Which livery stable?" Longarm asked.

"The one across from the New International Hotel."

"How long ago was this?"

"At least a week."

Longarm thanked Sarah Farnsworth and the madam. Then he turned to Rosemary. "Let's go."

Obviously relieved that Longarm was through with them, Madam Julie dismissed Sarah Farnsworth and escorted Longarm and Rosemary from her house. As they hurried along the crowded sidewalk a moment later, Rosemary shook her head.

"Poor Jane-Marie!" she exclaimed. "Imagine living in a stable!"

They found the owner of the livery at the rear of the place, cleaning out a stall. He was a small, balding ex-cowpoke who looked at least sixty. When Rosemary finished her description of Jane-Marie, he nodded quickly.

"Yep," he said. "I remember *her*, all right."

"Can you tell us where to find her?" asked Longarm.

"Guess maybe I can, at that."

"Well?"

"She's workin' at Ma Moon's parlor house on Magnolia Street."

"Since when?"

"Since she got enough money to fix herself up," the owner replied.

"You mean after she sold the ambulance."

"You mean after I helped her sell that foolish-lookin' circus wagon she rode in on. I was the one put the notice in the paper for her and took care of her till she sold it."

"And I assume you made sure you were well compensated for your help," Longarm suggested coldly.

The old cowpoke glanced nervously at Rosemary, then back at Longarm, a sudden grin on his face. If it were not for the gaps in his yellow teeth, he would have looked almost young again.

"All right. I admit it. Sure. She did an old man a favor. But she ain't feelin' no pain now, from what I been hearin'. Ma Moon was real happy to get her."

"Thank you," Rosemary said icily.

She took Longarm's arm and pulled him away, back toward the livery's entrance. Longarm thanked the livery-stable owner, turned, and left the stable with Rosemary.

"That horrid little man," Rosemary said as soon as they had gained the sidewalk outside. "He took advantage of Jane-Marie. Poor girl!"

"I'd say they took advantage of each other."

"Have it your way," Rosemary replied shortly.

"Do you want to come with me to Ma Moon's?"

She frowned. "No. Not this time, Longarm. That last place upset me so. I don't know what I had imagined these parlor houses would be like, but I'm simply not up to visiting another one. I'll wait for you both in my hotel room. It won't take long, will it?"

"Not if Jane-Marie's there—and this ain't another false alarm."

"Oh, I don't think it is. Not this time."

97

"Well, if not," he told her, "I should be back with Jane-Marie as soon as she can pack."

"Then do hurry, Longarm," she said fervently.

Longarm escorted Rosemary across the crowded street and, leaving her in the hotel lobby, hurried back out and headed for Magnolia Street.

Ma Moon was well named. She was as round as a silver dollar, with white hair and a glowing countenance. She wore a pale white gown cut deep enough to reveal a more than ample cleavage. She greeted Longarm with open arms and was already escorting him to the front parlor to meet her girls before Longarm managed to get his badge out and explain the nature of his visit.

"Oh, dear me," said Ma, pulling up in some confusion. "You're sure Sarah's not in some kind of trouble?"

"On the contrary. If she's the girl I'm looking for, her troubles should be over."

"You mean she's come into some money—an inheritance?"

Longarm smiled. "Something like that."

"It sounds so mysterious!" Ma's eyes gleamed.

"I'm sure Sarah will want to share her good fortune with you when she hears it."

"All right then," Ma said, her eyes still glowing. "I'll bring her down. But I must confess, if she leaves here, I'll miss her—and so will many of my best clients. She was fitting in so nicely."

"Is there someplace where we could talk? I have a lot to explain to her if she's the right girl."

"Of course," Ma said, taking him by the sleeve and guiding him through a narrow passageway, then through a red-paneled door. He found himself in a two-room apartment with a large desk and couch in the room he was entering, a canopied bed in the adjoining room, the curtains enclosing it a brilliant scarlet.

"This is my apartment," Ma said. "You can talk here in complete privacy. I'll go get Sarah now."

"It might help," Longarm told her, "if you didn't mention what I just told you—or that I'm a federal marshal. If she's the wrong girl, it wouldn't do to get her hopes up."

"Of course, Marshal."

As Ma Moon vanished out the door, Longarm slumped on the couch and took out a cheroot. He was on his first couple of puffs when he heard the door open behind him. He got up and turned.

Jane-Marie entered, and this time Longarm was not disappointed. Tall and willowy, she was a stunning woman with wide blue eyes, full, passionate lips, and long, shimmering blond hair that cascaded down past her shoulders. Her simple blue shift clung to her figure, revealing a generous bosom and the waist of a girl in her teens. On her manicured feet she wore open sandals. For a moment Longarm was reminded of a mural he had once seen of a procession of Greek goddesses.

No wonder she had become a favorite at Ma Moon's parlor house.

As Jane-Marie pulled the door shut behind her, she looked questioningly at Longarm. "Mr. Long?" she inquired.

He smiled. "Yes. And you're Sarah?"

"I am."

"Or could it be Jane-Marie?"

She uttered a tiny gasp. "What . . . whatever do you mean?"

"I'm sorry. I didn't want to alarm you."

"But you know who I am!"

"Yes."

"And you haven't come to arrest me?"

"No," he assured her, smiling. "You have nothing to fear

99

from that business in England."

"I . . . I don't know what you mean."

"It's all right. Really. You don't have to worry any longer. Your fiancé did not die. He recovered nicely."

"Then I am no longer wanted by the police?"

"No."

"And you've come all this way to tell me that?"

"No, that's not why I have been sent to find you. There's something else."

"Oh?" she asked, her voice barely audible. "And what would that be?"

"You are now the Duchess of Clyde."

"Me?" Jane-Marie was astonished. "But . . . but how could *that* be?" And then sudden realization flooded over her face. Her face paled and she took a short step back. "My brother! Has something happened to him?"

Longarm nodded.

"He's . . . dead?"

"Yes."

"And his wife, Evelyn? And little Robbie and Clarissa?"

"It was a boating accident. They were all drowned."

"Oh, my God! All of them . . . dead!"

Longarm nodded. Jane-Marie looked as if she needed to sit down. He hurried to her side and helped her sit down on the couch, chiding himself for having broken the news to her so abruptly.

"I'm sorry," he said. "I should have held off telling you this with so little preparation."

"I'm all right," Jane-Marie managed. Then she smiled wanly and looked up at him. "But I think perhaps I could use a drink."

"Brandy?"

She nodded.

Longarm went to the door and looked out. Ma Moon

was standing at the end of the narrow corridor, waiting anxiously. Longarm beckoned her to him and asked her to bring in some brandy. The woman turned and hurried off.

Returning to the room, Longarm closed the door behind him. "Perhaps I'd better start at the beginning."

"Yes," Jane-Marie agreed, taking a deep breath. "If you would, please."

When Longarm had finished telling her about the boating accident and how he had been sent to find her, not failing to mention Rosemary, Jane-Marie smiled brilliantly.

Eyes glowing, she cried, "You mean Rosemary's here? In Digger Falls?"

Longarm smiled and nodded. "She's waiting for you right now at the hotel."

"And I can go back! I can return home!"

"Yes. Home to England."

Ma Moon came in at that moment carrying a tray containing a bottle of brandy and three glasses. Ma was evidently eager to join them. They let her pour, and once they were each holding a glass of brandy, Longarm cleared his throat.

"I suggest a toast," he said, "to the new Duchess of Clyde!" As he spoke, he lifted the glass to Jane-Marie.

"The Duchess of Clyde!" Ma exclaimed. "How wonderful! Just think. One of my girls a duchess!"

"Yes," Jane-Marie responded, a rueful frown suddenly creasing her forehead. "One of your girls."

Suddenly sobered, the three drank up.

An hour or so later, Longarm entered the New International Hotel with Jane-Marie, carrying her single light suitcase. He went at once to the desk clerk, put down the suitcase, and asked him to send a bellboy up to fetch Miss Sutcliff.

"Miss Sutcliff is not in her room, Mr. Long," the clerk

said, indicating her room key resting in her mailbox. "I saw her leave myself about an hour ago."

Longarm thanked the clerk and turned to Jane-Marie. "We can wait for Rosemary on the veranda," he told her. "It will give us more time to get acquainted."

"That would be nice," she said.

As the desk clerk took charge of Jane-Marie's luggage, they walked out onto the hotel porch and found two wicker chairs in a quiet corner. Settling into them, they ordered lemonade. As they waited for the drinks, Longarm peered with a slight frown at the crowds surging along the sidewalk. Where had Rosemary gone, he wondered, and where was she now? She had said she would be waiting anxiously for their arrival. So why wasn't she here?

"Something is bothering you, Mr. Long," Jane-Marie said.

"Not really."

"You expected to find Rosemary waiting here. And now you don't know where she is."

He looked at her and laughed. "I guess I'll have to admit it."

"Don't worry about Rosemary."

"Oh?"

"I've known her all my life. She's a cousin on my mother's side, but we've been more like sisters."

"That so?"

Jane-Marie nodded. "And she's *such* fun to be with. Men find her quite attractive, I understand."

"Is that so?"

"Oh, yes. Rosemary's a very exciting person—and *very* unpredictable." Jane-Marie leaned back and laughed delightedly as she recalled some escapade out of Rosemary's past. "She gets into such terrible scrapes at times! Yet somehow she always manages to land on her feet."

"Like a cat."

"Yes." She sobered then. "I only hope I can be that lucky."

"Seems to me you've done just that, from what I gather."

"You know all about me, then."

Longarm shrugged. "I know pretty much."

The lemonade came. He wished he had ordered something a mite stronger.

"I am not asking you to forgive me," Jane-Marie said. "I told myself I had no other choice. But of course I did. I guess I just didn't care what happened to me or what I became. Can you understand that, Mr. Long?"

"No, ma'am, I cannot. Not for myself, that is."

"No, I suppose not," she said, looking away, her eyes troubled.

"Take my advice," Longarm told her gently, "and put it all behind you. Soon you'll be back in England and you can start up where you left off."

She looked at him quickly, then laughed, leaning her head back. "Oh, I wouldn't want to do *that*, Mr. Long!"

He grinned at her, pleased to see how quickly she was able to regain her spirits. "No," he agreed. "I suppose not."

"But I *am* glad I did not hurt Percival seriously. He is really such a poor excuse for a gentleman. Looking back now, I don't know what in the world I could ever have seen in him." She shook her head. "It seems so unreal now— almost like a dream."

He said nothing and smiled to encourage her to go on. It was obvious she was anxious to unburden herself.

"This country of yours is real enough, though," she went on, shuddering slightly. "And cruel! You have no idea what terrible things I have seen in this Wild West of yours!" She shook her head. "This is a very violent country, Mr. Long."

"I've noticed," Longarm said.

As gently as he could, he asked her about Leadville and her flight from Frankie Paige's parlor house. What she told him confirmed his own suspicions. Big Bill Barnstable had been Frankie Paige's lover, but he had grown weary of Frankie and began casting eyes in Jane-Marie's direction. Though Jane-Marie did her best not to encourage the man, there was a quarrel between him and Frankie, and in a fit of rage, Frankie Paige killed Big Bill with two shots from her pocket Smith and Wesson.

Unfortunately, Jane-Marie was a witness. So Frankie paid a sizable sum to Doc Hamlet, who was resting up in the parlor house at the time, to dispose of Barnstable's body and at the same time to kidnap and later kill Jane-Marie. She was bound hand and foot and dumped into the ambulance alongside Barnstable's dead body, after which Doc Hamlet rode out of Leadville. Later, Hamlet found himself unwilling to kill Jane-Marie as he had promised Frankie Paige.

"I do not deny it," Jane-Marie said bleakly. "I found ways to dissuade him."

Longarm nodded without comment as Jane-Marie continued, telling how she became a more or less trusted member of Doc Hamlet's "family." When she began taking part in the nightly shows and demonstrations, it became obvious that her presence beside Doc Hamlet during his pitch insured a large turnout and a considerable increase in sales.

"Then one day," Jane-Marie said, "Hamlet spent an entire afternoon adding to the bottles a new herb or whatever it was he had found. I asked him what he was doing. He said he was giving the elixir a kick. Well, that night I noticed what that new kick did to one woman. I tried to warn him, but he wouldn't listen."

"So you ran out on him and Will Clay."

"Yes. I took the wagon and drove off with it. That was

104

the only way I could think of to stop him. I was frightened, Custis. There was already some commotion in the town, something about a very sick town marshal."

"You'd be interested to know that the town marshal died, and that the townspeople almost lynched Hamlet and Clay."

"But they escaped?"

Longarm nodded somewhat bleakly. "With my help, I must admit. You see, they were the only lead I had on where you might have gone."

"I see. Well, as soon as I could, I destroyed ever single bottle in that wagon and kept going until I reached here."

"But not before stopping at a small ranch on the way."

She looked at him in surprise. "You know about that too?"

"I stopped at the same ranch on my way here. That was a fine thing you did."

"What else could I do?" she said, shrugging. "I've had some experience nursing cholera victims. How are the Perkinses?"

"They were all up and about except for the youngest child."

She smiled, obviously pleased at this news. Longarm leaned back in his chair and regarded Jane-Marie for a moment or two, a slight frown on his face.

She looked at him quizzically. "What are you thinking?" she asked.

"I'm thinking about Frankie Paige and Doc Hamlet. She got away with murder, and Hamlet was an accessory."

"I know."

"Would you be willing to return to Leadville to help me nail that madam, at least?"

"Do you think we could?"

He nodded emphatically.

"All right, then."

"Good. If all goes well, we'll stop at Leadville on our way back to Denver."

At that moment a cry came from the porch steps to their right. Longarm turned as Rosemary swept up the steps and rushed toward Jane-Marie, her arms outstretched. Jane-Marie jumped up and the two old friends embraced each other fiercely, both of them laughing and talking at the same time. The other guests seated on the porch watched their reunion with unmistakable pleasure, their eyes alight with almost the same level of excitement that animated the two girls.

Longarm gave Rosemary his chair so the two could talk, then excused himself and went into the hotel. He had Jane-Marie's bag sent up to Rosemary's room, then left the hotel and walked down the street to the telegraph office. He wired Vail, informing him of his success in tracking down Jane-Marie and of his intention to stop off at Leadville on his return.

Then he pushed into a crowded saloon next door, purchased a bottle of Maryland rye, and sat himself down in a corner, his back to the wall. At an unhurried, deliberate pace, his brow furrowed, he poured himself his first drink.

Back in his room that night, Longram had almost dropped off when he heard light footsteps in the hallway outside his door. A soft knock followed. He threw back the covers and padded across the room on bare feet.

Leaning his head against the door, he asked, "Who is it?"

"It's me, Longarm. Rosemary!"

He turned the key and opened the door. Rosemary was in her nightgown, her long hair combed out, her eyes gleaming with anticipation. When he smiled, she stepped into his arms. He pulled her in and closed the door behind her. He had been expecting just such a visit.

"I came to thank you," Rosemary told him softly, "for all you've done."

Then she went up on tiptoes and kissed him full on the lips. He returned her kiss, then led her over to his bed.

As before, he made no effort to light his dresser lamp and in no time at all he had stripped Rosemary, whose own deft fingers were fast stroking his hot poker to life. He bore her down beneath him, covering her shoulders and breasts with kisses. Clinging hungrily to him, she twined her long limbs about his slim torso. His lips enflamed her breasts, then her belly as he moved still farther down. She became frantic.

Uttering tiny cries of delight, she pulled him to her and closed her lips about his own throbbing manhood. Her wanton expertise was almost too much for him. Swiftly he moved atop her, and with his big hands reaching under her, grabbed her buttocks and slammed her up into him. As he felt himself entering, he lunged down heavily, impaling her on the bed beneath him.

"Yes," she cried, laughing. "Oh, yes!"

"You like that?" he muttered.

"More! Go deeper! Much deeper!"

He complied, driving harder with each thrust. Clinging to him excitedly, she leaned her head back and flung her pelvis upward, moaning and grinding her teeth with each frantic lunge. By this time, neither of them were calculating human beings. They were simply animals in heat, aware of nothing but the mad, driving lust that had caught them up in its fierce, pounding rhythm, sending them over the edge at last into a sweet oblivion, a kind of sad, lovely emptiness.

"Mmmm," Rosemary murmured contentedly when she had gotten her breath back. She rested her head on his shoulder, her fingers tracing a design through the thick, coiled hair on his chest. "That was nice. So very nice."

Longarm nodded.

She reached down, then laughed. "You are a marvel, Longarm—and so well named!"

He reached over with his big, gentle hand and closed it about the fullness of her breast, his thumb flicking over the nipple. She leaned back and sighed. He took his hand away and closed his mouth over the nipple. A moment later his tongue was driving her slowly wild as her body undulated lascivously under him. Then, moving silkily, she slid out from under him and positioned herself atop him.

Like old friends, they traveled together over familiar territory. He leaned back, stretching to his full length as he allowed her to lower herself down upon him. As her hot, soaking lips closed like a fist about his erection, the warmth of her was almost enough to set him off.

She began to move then, so slowly and delicately that for a moment or two he was almost lulled to sleep as she rocked gently back and forth. But then with a deep, seductive laugh, she awakened him swiftly as she began to rotate her hips with a maddening, voluptuous expertise that caused something deep within his groin to come ferociously alive.

With a deep muttering cry he reached out for her breasts. Laughing softly, she leaned closer so he could take them in his hands, all the while continuing her deft, maddening rotating motion. They built swiftly then to a mutual climax, after which she flung herself happily forward into his arms. For a long, delicious moment, they clung to each other. Then he rolled her off him.

"Now, how was that?" she asked impishly.

"Fine."

"That's how I say thank you," she told him softly, kissing him lightly on the lips.

"How's Jane-Marie?"

"Very happy. She has all kinds of plans for the estate—

and for her first ball of the upcoming season."

"And, of course, you're invited."

Rosemary smiled. "Yes. And you too—if you could make the trip."

"I am afraid not," Longarm murmured, allowing his voice to drop off, as if he were close to sleep.

Rosemary rested her head on his chest and closed her eyes. After a while, her breathing became heavier and more regular. Longarm closed his own eyes and pretended to sleep.

Rosemary was very patient. For a long while she lay with her head on his chest, breathing regularly, heavily. At last she stirred, then lifted her head off Longarm's chest and studied him closely for a minute or two.

Then she leaned still closer and whispered his name.

Longarm did not respond.

At last, certain he was asleep, she slowly, carefully pushed herself back off the bed. As she stood up, she kept both hands on the mattress, then gently let up on it so that it would not jounce and awaken Longarm.

He continued to breathe steadily. He could feel her standing over him, watching. Then he heard her soft footfalls on the rug and the sound of her silken nightgown slipping over her head, after which she moved swiftly around to the other side of the bed. Through slitted eyes, he watched her reach carefully in under the pillow for his Colt. With a deftness that surprised him, she unloaded the .44, dropped the cartridges into her nightgown pocket, then replaced the empty weapon back in under his pillow.

For a long moment she stood watching him. He wondered what she was thinking. Perhaps she was sorry to have to do this. He doubted it. For his part, he was relieved. He had been wondering for some time when she was going to make her move.

Backing carefully to the door, she opened it, slipped out, then closed it softly behind her.

He waited until the sound of her footsteps faded completely. Then he snatched his gunbelt from the bedpost and swiftly reloaded the Colt. Slipping back off the bed, he fluffed up the sheets and blanket, using one of the two pillows to simulate his shoulder, after which he dropped down behind the bed.

He did not have long to wait.

Heavy footsteps approached the door. A boot crashed against it, swinging it wide. In the doorway, silhouetted against the wall lamp, stood two men, their shapes vaguely familiar. Charging into the room, they thrust out their revolvers and fired repeatedly at the dummy figure Longarm had provided for them.

As the thunderous detonations shook the tiny room, filling the air with clouds of acrid smoke, Longarm fired from under the bed at the man closest. The round punched into his gut belt-high. The gunman buckled and let his heavy weapon clatter to the floor. In some confusion, his companion spun and glanced down at the floor. With one arm holding the bed's frame, Longarm swung out from under the bed, firing coolly up into the second gunman's face, stamping a dark hole under his right eye. The man toppled loosely to the floor.

Pulling himself out from under the bed, Longarm caught movement on his right and saw the head and shoulders of a third gunman thrusting forward through the window into the room. Longarm recognized him at once as the member of Jim Blade's gang who had been waiting for him on the canyon's rim. Longarm swung his gun around quickly and fired. The round missed. The window above the outlaw's head disintegrated as he returned Longarm's fire, his round smashing the revolver out of Longarm's hand. When Longarm reached down for it, the outlaw strode swiftly forward and kicked the gun out of his reach.

As Longarm fumbled in his vest pocket for his derringer, a tall, familiar figure materialized in the doorway and a rifle cracked sharply. The bullet crashed into the gunman's back and he crumpled like an empty sack to the floor at Longarm's feet. Peering through the shifting coils of gunsmoke, Longarm saw Old Buffalo joining Bolt in the doorway.

Bolt and the Indian had overtaken him, just as Bolt had promised—so, once again, Longarm owed his life to the Englishman.

Chapter 9

The hallway outside Longarm's room was filled rapidly with curious guests. Longarm pulled Bolt and Old Buffalo into the room and slammed his door shut.

"Where the hell did you two come from?" he demanded as he lit the dresser lamp and started to dress.

"We just rode in," Bolt told him. "The desk clerk gave us your room number. I'd say we got here not a minute too soon."

"I am much obliged."

"Did you find Sarah Smith?"

"I did. But her name isn't Sarah Smith." Longarm looked carefully at Bolt. "Her name is Jane-Marie."

Bolt did not bat an eye. "And is she in good health?"

Shrugging into his frock coat, Longarm reloaded his Colt and dropped it into his cross-draw rig. "She's in excellent health. That is, she was the last time I saw her."

Slamming on his hat, Longarm stepped over the nearest

dead outlaw and started for the door. But before he reached it, the door burst open and the town marshal stormed in, the hotel manager and the desk clerk right behind him. The town marshal was an older, stocky man with gray temples and a hard, weathered face. His chin was solid and his eyes gave no hint of backing off.

"Hold it right there!" the town marshal cried, addressing the three men. "Just where in blazes do you all think you're going?"

"Just down the hall, Marshal," Longarm told him. "And I'd be obliged if you'd just get out of my way. I'm in a hurry."

As Longarm spoke, the town marshal caught sight of the three sprawled bodies. "Jesus . . . !" he whispered, passing a big, meaty hand across his face.

Swiftly, he bent to examine each man. They were all still warm, but as dead as fence posts.

"You three did this?" the town marshal asked warily, looking back up at Longarm and his two companions.

Longarm pointed to Bolt. "The two of us," he said.

"What the hell was it, anyway—a gambling debt?"

"They stormed the room and started blasting. My two friends here happened along at the tail end of it and lent a hand."

"What the hell kind of explanation is that? You mean these three just came in here without no warning and started shooting? For no reason—none at all?"

"That's what I said."

"Damn it! That don't make no kind of sense! You mean you never seen any one of these men before?"

"As a matter of fact, I do recall that one over there," Longarm said, pointing to the outlaw Bolt had shot. "But the others are all strangers to me."

"I think you better come downstairs to the lockup—all

three of you. Just for safekeeping, mind."

Longarm had been trying to get past the town marshal without showing his badge. He never liked to pull rank. But he saw he had no choice in the matter now. Reaching into his pocket, he took out his wallet and flashed his badge at the man. "I'm a deputy U. S. marshal," he told the lawman. "Let me by."

The town marshal was a stubborn man. "You mean the three of you are working for the federal government?" he demanded, stepping back in front of the open doorway.

"Just me," Longarm explained patiently. "But these two are with me."

The town marshal glanced uneasily at Old Buffalo. The big Indian stared back at him, his obsidian eyes unblinking. After a quick glance at Bolt, the town marshal looked back at Longarm. "Are these two in any official capacity?"

"I can deputize them if I want."

"What's your hurry to get out of here?"

"I've come a long way to find someone, and I just might have lost her again. She could be in her room down the hall. You can come with me if you want."

"You're damn right I will," the town marshal said, stepping to one side.

The first thing Longarm noticed as he left his room and pushed his way through the curious guests that clogged the hallway was that neither Rosemary nor Jane-Marie were among those frantically eager to investigate all the shooting. With a growing sense of unease, Longarm led Bolt and Old Buffalo down the hallway to Rosemary's room, the hotel manager and the desk clerk following. Reaching Rosemary's room, he saw at once that the door was ajar. With the toe of his boot, he nudged it open.

The room was empty. As he had feared, Rosemary and Jane-Marie were gone.

At least a dozen people outside the hotel remembered the four riders—two men and two women—who rode out of town only minutes before the gunfire erupted inside the hotel. One of the girls was definitely Jane-Marie. Her blonde hair made that impossible to deny. The other girl was, just as obviously, Rosemary, and as Longarm continued his questioning, he knew at once who the two men with them were: Jim Blade and his brother Tommy.

Before an hour had passed, Longarm, Bolt, and Old Buffalo were riding out of town, heading south. When dawn broke, they were approaching the pass, and it was not long before Old Buffalo picked up Blade's trail. The outlaw was heading for the pass.

The three riders pulled up on a slight crest later that day and saw, about a quarter of a mile ahead of them, the Perkins ranch. Four horses, still saddled, were standing at the hitch rack, their exhaustion mirrored eloquently in the weary droop of their heads.

"They're in there all right," Longarm observed gloomily, "but I don't like it."

"You worried about Sam Perkins and his family?"

Longarm nodded. "Them two outlaws won't be gentle with them, and if they catch us moving in, they'll sure as hell try to use them as hostages."

"Relax. Perkins and his family are staying with some neighbors on the other side of the pass. We took them there. They were too weak to do much for themselves. Right now the four of them are in the ranch house alone."

Old Buffalo spoke up then. "No. They not alone. Is with them white man's pestilence."

"By God," exclaimed Bolt. "He's bloody well right. And if any of them drink that water . . . !"

"Maybe better in ranch house we can keep them," Old

116

Buffalo suggested. "Let cholera empty their guts." He smiled then, the heavy folds in his face adjusting with remarkable speed.

Longarm shook his head emphatically. "Jane-Marie won't let that happen. She'll warn them and tell them to boil the water."

"Boil water no help," Old Buffalo rumbled.

Longarm looked back at the ranch house. Old Buffalo was probably right. Maybe boiling water and washing everything was effective in preventing the spread of cholera, but it was difficult to be sure. He'd heard of other cures just as wild, but when cholera struck, there wasn't much you could do except drink plenty of water, squat, and hope for the best.

"What do you suggest, Longarm?" Bolt asked.

"We wait until dark and then use the cottonwoods for cover. Maybe we can surprise them."

Bolt nodded. Longarm turned his horse back off the ridge, Bolt and Old Buffalo following.

It was close to dusk when the three of them reached the foot of the cottonwoods. The rear of the ranch house was less than forty feet from them. Occasionally they could hear the sound of voices coming from within the cabin.

They would have to wait until it got darker, Longarm decided. He hunkered down, then leaned back against the foot of a tree and took out his Colt to make sure of its load. Bolt and Old Buffalo scrunched down beside him and examined their weapons as well. Bolt still favored his Winchester, and Old Buffalo was carrying the Colt revolver Longarm had handed him after the stage holdup.

"As soon as it gets dark enough," Longarm said, "I'll see if I can't get through one of those rear windows. If I can surprise them, there won't be any need for gunfire. I

117

don't want to risk hitting the women. But if I need help, I'll let you know."

"One gunshot will do," Bolt said.

Longarm nodded. "But wait for that signal. Don't see why this shouldn't go real nice and quiet."

"What makes you think that?"

"Because they don't know anyone's on their tail. I'm supposed to be dead by now—killed by them three gun-slicks Rosemary set me up for. They never did wait to find out what happened."

Bolt nodded. "And so all Rosemary needs to do now is find a good excuse to get rid of Jane-Marie."

"Either that, or just abandon her somewhere. Leave her to rot."

"That would do it," Bolt agreed gloomily. "The College of Heralds has already waited pretty long. I am sure they would not find it difficult to settle on Rosemary as the sole surviving relative and make her the duchess."

Longarm looked back at the ranch house and took a deep breath.

He knew Bolt was probably right. Back in Digger Falls the Englishman had finally admitted what Longarm had long since surmised—that Bolt had known from the beginning who Sarah Smith really was.

Realizing that Bolt was in love with Jane-Marie and that she would have nothing more to do with him, Jane-Marie's now penitent ex-fiancé had urged Bolt to go after her to America and see to her safe return to England. Bolt had needed no urging. He had already decided to go after Rosemary when he learned that Jane-Marie's cousin was also leaving for America to find Jane-Marie.

Having no idea where Jane-Marie might be, Bolt simply followed Rosemary as she went first to New Orleans and then to Denver. Once he saw Rosemary with Longarm—a man he knew to be a deputy U. S. marshal—Bolt realized that Rosemary had enlisted the aid of the U. S. government in her search. He was still following her when her stage was held up.

When it appeared Rosemary had been kidnapped by Blade's gang, Bolt took the opportunity to join forces with Longarm and continue his search for the girl Longarm referred to as Sarah Smith, but whom he knew as Jane-Marie. The realization last night that Rosemary had been allied with Jim Blade all along came as a shock but not as a complete surprise, for he knew Rosemary to be a cold, ruthless woman, willing to do anything to make herself the Duchess of Clyde—a fact Longarm had realized himself the moment Jane-Marie revealed to him that Rosemary was her cousin.

Indeed, this fact had answered some nagging questions that had begun to plague Longarm. Why, for instance, had Longarm been singled out and almost killed during that stage holdup—and why had Rosemary herself been kidnapped? The answer was that Longarm's death and Rosemary's kidnapping had been planned beforehand, for with Longarm dead, Rosemary would be free, with Jim Blade's help, to find Jane-Marie on her own—and take whatever steps were necessary to prevent her cousin from returning to England.

With Longarm's unexpected survival, however, she and Blade had been forced to change their plans—and a way had to be found for her to rejoin Longarm. This explained why it had been so easy for Longarm to rescue Rosemary and why Blade's men had deliberately shown themselves on that ridge. It had been a clear invitation for him to scramble up that slope after them—and he had swallowed the bait, hook and all.

Longarm saw that it was now completely dark. He stood back and looked at Bolt and Old Buffalo.

119

"Let's get to it," he said. "You two move around to the front of the ranch house. If they make a break for it once I get in, you'll be able to stop them. But, like I said, don't do anything until you hear my signal."

The two nodded and moved out, Bolt going to one side of the ranch house, Old Buffalo to the other. When they had disappeared into the gloom, Longarm left the cotton-woods and slipped across the backyard and approached a dirt-encrusted window. Peering through it, he was able to make out a door leading into the next room. A faint sliver of light gleamed under it.

Using the barrel of his Colt, he pried up the sash until he was able to reach in and grab hold of it with both hands. Heaving upward, he boosted himself over the sill and into the room. It was a small storage room and it smelled of potatoes and flour. With gun drawn, he stepped over the sacks and approached the door.

With his gun barrel he nudged the door open a fraction of an inch and maneuvered himself so that he was able to see Jane-Marie. She was bound to a chair in a corner, a filthy rag tied around her mouth. Blade and his brother were sitting at a table playing cards. Blade's back was to Longarm. Longarm could see Tommy's face clearly as he frowned down at the hand Jim Blade had just dealt him. Behind Tommy, Rosemary sat on the edge of a cot, watching them. She seemed impatient and restless.

Not one of the three gave Jane-Marie a glance. It was almost as if she no longer existed.

Longarm kicked open the door.

Blade flung about in his seat. His brother jumped up, his right hand dropping to his sixgun.

"That would be foolish," Longarm told him, leveling his .44 on the man's chest.

120

"Longarm!" Rosemary cried, her face ashen. "But I thought—"

"No, I'm not dead, Rosemary," he told her. "Sorry to disappoint you."

"Why . . . whatever do you mean? Of course you're not dead! You don't know how pleased I am to see you! These two men abducted Jane-Marie and myself!"

Longarm smiled thinly, then aimed at the ceiling and pulled the trigger. As the detonation filled the room, the front door burst open and Bolt and Old Buffalo burst in. One look at Bolt and Rosemary clapped her hand over her mouth.

She knew Bolt, and she knew that Bolt knew her. In that instant, she realized that further protestations were useless.

"Untie Jane-Marie," Longarm told Rosemary.

As Rosemary hurried over to Jane-Marie, Longarm and Bolt disarmed the two brothers. Once free of the chair and the gag untied, Jane-Marie got unsteadily to her feet, glanced in some surprise at Bolt, then hurried over to Longarm.

"Marshal, I tried to warn them. But they wouldn't listen!"

"About the cholera?"

"Yes."

"I listened," said Rosemary coldly, a tiny smile glinting on her face. "But they just laughed and said it was a trick, that Jane-Marie was lying. They've been drinking the water and eating the food they found here. I wanted to move on as soon as Jane-Marie told them, but they wouldn't hear of it."

Longarm looked at both men. They were beginning to understand their mistake now. Cold sweat gleamed on their ashen faces.

"Jane-Marie was telling you the truth," Longarm told them. "The family living here all came down with the cholera. They're recovering now at a neighbor's. Maybe you should have listened." He waggled his sixgun at them. "All right. Move out of here. We got a ways to go yet."

"Where we goin'?" Jim Blade demanded. "Where you takin' us?"

"Leadville first, then Denver."

As the two men filed out of the ranch house with Rosemary, Old Buffalo following them with his cocked weapon, Jane-Marie turned to Alfred Bolt.

"What a surprise to see *you* here, Alfred! What on earth are you doing so far from home?" Her voice was correct but icy.

"That's a long story."

"Well, you must tell me all about it some day," she told him, as she swept past him into the night.

Bolt looked unhappily at Longarm and shrugged. Then he followed Jane-Marie out of the ranch house. He had to go slow, as he had already told Longarm, since Jane-Marie knew him as a friend of Percival Warren—and any friend of her ex-fiancé was no friend of Jane-Marie's.

Indeed, her lack of warmth toward Bolt did not surprise Longarm. By now Jane-Marie had had a bellyful of old friends from England.

Chapter 10

A full day later, Longarm made camp beside a stream some distance from the Perkins ranch. When they continued on toward Leadville the next day, Longarm was careful to give the town of Blackwood a wide berth. Though the detour made the journey considerably longer, Longarm saw no alternative. As far as Blackwood's citizens were concerned, not only did Longarm free two murderers, but two horse thieves as well.

A day later, along about sunset, as they were making camp, Longarm noticed how poorly Tommy Blade looked.

Longarm walked over to Bolt. "I'm thinking we'd best let those two camp away from us," he said.

Bolt nodded grimly. "I've been noticing the young blighter. I recognize that peaked look of his all too well. I think that would be a very good idea, Longarm."

Longarm walked over to Jane-Marie, who was busy unfolding her soogan. "Looks like young Blade is coming down with the cholera. If he does, I don't want you going near him."

"I assure you, Marshal, I shall do nothing of the sort. He and his brother ignored my warning. Now let him suffer the consequences. I have no sympathy for his sort."

Longarm nodded. "Good. We just might have to leave both of them if it gets any worse, and I wouldn't want you to give me any argument."

"I will not protest."

Longarm left Jane-Marie and walked over to the two brothers. Since that morning, Longarm had allowed them to ride without having their wrists bound. As Longarm stopped before them, Tommy Blade remained sitting on the ground, a sick haggard look on his face, blue patches under both eyes.

"I think you two better make a separate camp some distance from the rest of us," Longarm said.

Looking fearfully up at Longarm, Tommy Blade licked his parched lips nervously. "You think I got it, don't you?" he whined.

"Yes," said Longarm. "I do."

"Damn you! Damn you all to hell!"

Longarm looked back at Jim Blade. "You heard me. Move your things away from this camp."

Nodding miserably, Jim Blade took up his soogan and saddle and moved off. His brother watched him go for a moment or two. Then, groaning, he got to his feet, grabbed his gear, and trailed after his brother. In a moment the two had disappeared into a stand of cottonwoods a good hundred yards away.

Watching them disappear, Longarm felt nothing—not even pity.

Old Buffalo pulled up beside him. "Good thing is that. Old Buffalo ready he to leave soon when see how outlaw look."

Rosemary approached. Her look was sullen. "You aren't

going to send me away too, are you?" she asked.

"Not unless you come down with it too."

"You mean that, don't you? You *would* send me away."

"Of course. For the sake of the others."

She shuddered. "And after all the . . . consideration I showed you."

Longarm laughed. "Is that what you call it?"

As Rosemary's face darkened in sudden fury, he turned and left her.

The next morning, Longarm noticed Jane-Marie was no longer keeping Bolt at arm's length and was allowing the Englishman to pack her sleeping bag while she made the coffee. Leaving them, Longarm walked into the cotton-woods in search of Jim Blade and his brother.

He found them lying half-naked under a pine. Tommy had fouled himself during the night and flung his pants and underdrawers some distance from him. He was sicker by far than his brother, and as he stared miserably up at Long-arm, his teeth chattered fiercely from the chills that were ravaging him. There was a look of pure animal terror in his eyes.

"We're pulling out," Longarm told Jim Blade. "I heard somewhere you should drink plenty of water, so it might be a good idea to get back to that stream. We'll leave you what food we can."

"You mean you're just gonna *leave* us?"

"It's the best chance you'll get. If either of you makes it, you'll be free. Otherwise you'll rot in Yuma."

"But we'll die if you leave us!" cried Tommy.

"That ain't a certainty. There's some pull through this. You'll just have to take your chances like everybody else."

"You bastard!"

Longarm stared down at them for a moment without

replying, his cold eyes unwavering. Then he turned and left them, their ragged, bitter curses following after him.

When Longarm emerged from the timber, he saw Old Buffalo talking to Bolt. When the Indian saw Longarm, he left the Englishman and led his horse toward Longarm. From the solemn look on the old Indian's face, Longarm sensed what was coming.

Halting, Longarm greeted the Indian.

"Old Buffalo must go now," he told Longarm. "Glad I am not to die of white man's sickness. I go now to the lodges of my people. Their voices hear I in the wind and in the tall grasses of the hills. They speak to me. They call to me. So I go."

"Then go in peace, Old Buffalo."

"Yes. I go in peace. But not if still must I be prisoner inside white man's agency. Old Buffalo is not agency Indian."

Longarm nodded in agreement. "You are right. Old Buffalo is not an agency Indian. And he is a friend of Longarm."

Old Buffalo beamed. "Glad is my heart to hear your words. To my lodge one day you must come. We will hunt together."

The Indian mounted up. Despite the checked vest and derby hat, his bearing was impressive and dignified. With a single wave he rode off, heading toward a distant line of hills. As Longarm watched him go, he felt suddenly poorer and a good deal lonelier.

Rosemary hurried toward him. She had kept her distance while Jane-Marie made breakfast that morning, and Longarm had seen her refuse a cup of coffee Jane-Marie had offered her. Now she planted herself before Longarm, her bold chin thrust out defiantly.

"I just saw you leave the woods. Did you find Jim and Tommy?"

"I found them."

"Are they very sick?"

"I guess you could say that."

"Will they die?" Rosemary asked.

"Maybe."

"What are you going to do?"

"There's nothing any of us can do except leave them what food we can."

Rosemary smiled, her eyes narrowing shrewdly. "Of course you realize that without Jim or Tommy Blade to testify against me, you have no proof I was working with them. If you insist on bringing charges against me, I'll deny it—every bit of it."

She was right, Longarm realized. Without those two brothers, he had no case against her.

Rosemary's dark blue eyes glittered in triumph. "And once I am back in England, do you really think I will allow Jane-Marie to become the next Duchess of Clyde—after what I tell the authorities?"

Jane-Marie and Bolt had been listening. "Rosemary," Jane-Marie broke in, her voice hushed, "what are you going to tell them?"

Rosemary flung about to face Jane-Marie, her eyes flashing defiance. "You mean you really don't know?"

"Out with it!" demanded Bolt.

"I'll tell the truth, that's all. That the Duchess of Clyde is wanted not only for robbing a noted madam, Frankie Paige, but also for the murder of one of her customers, Bill Barnstable."

"Why, that's absurd!" Jane-Marie cried. "I never took a thing from Frankie—and I certainly had nothing to do with Bill Barnstable's death."

"Perhaps when we reach Leadville, you'll be able to convince Frankie Paige of your innocence, but I doubt it!"

Rosemary smiled at Jane-Marie in sudden triumph. "You see, Jane-Marie, I have all the cards now."

"My God, Rosemary," Jane-Marie cried. "What have I ever done to make you hate me so?"

"Nothing—except be a Darnsforth. It is really *quite* simple. What you have, I want. And I intend to get it!"

As Rosemary stalked off, Longarm remembered her earlier description of Jane-Marie. She had called her passionate and willful, insisting Jane-Marie was headstrong enough to defy a king.

Though Rosemary might not have realized it, she had really been describing herself.

That evening they made camp in a patch of timber beside a stream. As the four of them settled into their sleeping bags for the night, Bolt walked over to Longarm and hunkered down beside him. He was carrying his rifle.

"I want to talk to you about Jane-Marie and me," Bolt said.

"Talk."

"You know Jane-Marie had nothing to do with killing that fellow Barnstable."

"That's right."

"Then you can't take her back to Leadville. It will be Jane-Marie's word against Frankie Paige's, and Rosemary will be more than eager to testify against her as well."

"If Jane-Marie is innocent, she has to be cleared."

"But suppose the sheriff jails her?"

"It won't be pleasant. But if Jane-Marie does not clear herself, she'll never be the next Duchess of Clyde. Rosemary will see to that."

"It doesn't matter. None of that matters now."

"What the hell do you mean by that?"

"Jane-Marie no longer has any use for that title. She has me."

Longarm shook his head in wonder. He was always amazed at the foolish things people in love said and then compounded by believing.

"Well now, if Jane-Marie told you that, Bolt, I'm sure she means it. But time has a way of changing things. You sure she's going to feel the same way a year from now?"

"Of course she will. And so will I."

"You're a fool, Bolt."

"It's no use, Longarm. We've made up our minds. Jane-Marie is not going back to Leadville and a possible murder indictment."

As Bolt spoke, he stood up and pointed his rifle down at Longarm, his face now grim with resolve.

"Put that rifle away, Bolt."

"I mean it, Longarm. Jane-Marie is going with me. It's the way she wants it—and the way I want it. Don't try to stop us."

"I'm promising nothing, Bolt. Jane-Marie deserves that title and a chance to return home. And I intend to see that she gets both."

"We'll see about that," Bolt said, reaching deftly under Longarm's saddle for Longarm's Colt. He slipped it easily from its holster.

Longarm's derringer was in his vest, which he had folded neatly beside his saddle. But Longarm liked Bolt too much to take a chance on injuring him, fool though he was.

Producing a length of rawhide from his coat pocket, Bolt tied Longarm's wrists together behind his back, then bound both ankles with the same length of rawhide, trussing Longarm as neatly as a Thanksgiving turkey.

"I'll drop your gun in the grass over there," Bolt said,

indicating a spot near the stream.

He turned and hurried off, tossing the gun away as he did so. A moment later Longarm heard Bolt and Jane-Marie galloping off. He swore bitterly, futilely—then did something he hated to do. He called out to Rosemary for help.

But there was no answer.

Close to dawn that morning, his wrists bloody from his grueling and painful struggle to free himself, he found that while Bolt had dealt with Longarm, Jane-Marie had taken care of Rosemary, binding and gagging her with the same efficiency.

When Longarm finally cut her loose, he found himself dealing with a woman madder than a drunken squaw.

Chapter 11

By the time Longarm had retrieved his gun, Rosemary had calmed down somewhat and had built a fire for their breakfast. He sat wearily down beside the campfire and watched her fill the coffeepot. After she set the pot down in the coals, she brushed an unruly lock of hair off her forehead and looked over at him.

"I say good riddance," she said.

"That so?"

"She's done us both a favor, riding off with that fool."

"I was wondering when you'd realize that."

"So I say let her go."

"If she doesn't want the title, you do. That it?" he asked.

"Why not?"

Longarm looked at Rosemary for a long moment, then decided against trying to explain to her why not. Rosemary would simply not understand. Worse, she would not *want* to understand. Rosemary was thinking only of herself, while Longarm was trying to think not only of completing the mission Vail had sent him on, but of saving Jane-Marie as well. She and Bolt were sure as hell acting like fools, but at least—unlike Rosemary—it was not greed driving them.

"Never mind, Rosemary," Longarm said wearily. "It won't do any good to argue."

She handed him a cup of coffee. "You're going after them?"

"I am."

"Then I'm coming, too."

"You'd be better off going on to Leadville. You can catch a stage there for Denver."

"No. I'm going with you."

"You'll only slow me down."

"This is not friendly country, Longarm. How long do you think I'd last traveling alone? Don't you care at all about my safety?"

"Then come with me. But I am going to be traveling fast."

"But not too fast, I hope, to rest now and then." A faint smile hovered over her lips.

Finishing his coffee, Longarm stood up. He realized that, in spite of himself, he was no longer angry with Rosemary.

"I'm not promising anything," he told her. "Let's go."

By mid-afternoon, two days later, they followed Jane-Marie and Bolt's trail to Iron Creek, a small mining town which had clearly seen better days.

The mill's ore crushers on the hill above the town were still booming, but the beat was slow and ominous and the town had the appearance of a gentleman of means who had taken to wearing threadbare coats and unblocked hats. Evidence of decline was everywhere, from the deserted saloons and stores to the fact that only one hotel was still open.

They left their horses in the livery, then registered in the

Majestic Hotel next door. Flashing his badge, Longarm checked the register. He saw that no couples and no man and woman registering separately had registered in the past twenty-four hours. The Majestic was not doing so well, it seemed. Despite Rosemary's protests, Longarm registered for both of them, and took a room separate from hers.

"That's all right," she told him softly, as he stopped by the door to his room and inserted the key. "It isn't all that far for you to go—just two doors down."

He turned the key. "Don't count on it."

Pausing before her own room, she raised an eyebrow. "But, Longarm, it'll be so much nicer now—on clean sheets."

Longarm entered his room and dumped his gear on the bed. He hated to admit it, but Rosemary had a point.

He finished stowing his gear. Then, needing a haircut and a hot bath, he went looking for a barbershop and found one across the street from the town's biggest saloon, after which he crossed to the saloon to wet his whistle and make a few inquiries.

He was lucky enough to purchase a bottle of Maryland rye. He found a table in a corner and was lighting his second cheroot when the town marshal—a lean, rawboned fellow in his late twenties with a star pinned to his vest—finished his poker game and started from the place.

"Marshal?"

The lawman paused and looked in Longarm's direction. Longarm raised the bottle of Maryland rye and smiled.

"Get a glass and join me," Longarm said.

Curious, the marshal did as Longarm suggested. As soon as he was comfortable, Longarm told him who he was.

"Name's Tom Fogarty," the fellow responded, shaking Longarm's hand. "What can I do for you, Long?"

"I'm looking for a man and a woman who should have

133

ridden into Iron Creek sometime yesterday or early this morning."

"Can you describe them?"

Longarm could and did.

"What're they wanted for?"

"For being damned fools," Longarm replied. "It's a long story."

"Well, then, it ain't over yet."

"What do you mean by that?"

"They got married yesterday. Reverend Lighthorse did the honors."

Longarm was not really surprised. "That so?"

The town marshal nodded and downed his drink.

"Where are they staying?" Longarm asked.

"I'm not sure."

"Come on, Fogarty. Level with me."

"The rooming house on Cedar Hill, I think. Say, what's this all about, Long? Them two sure as hell didn't look like criminals to me—and not to anyone else."

"I didn't say they were."

Fogarty peered closely at Longarm. "Sure is strange, a deputy U. S. marshal goin' to all this trouble just to bring in a couple of harmless lovebirds."

Longarm got to his feet. "Much obliged, Marshal."

"Don't think nothin' of it." The town marshal smiled. "By the way, could I have a little more of that rye? It sure is smooth."

Longarm left the bottle with him.

The rooming-house door was opened by a cadaverous, dark-eyed fellow past fifty. He was holding a broom. His gaunt face was streaked with sweat and rings of sooty grime circled his scrawny neck.

"You lookin' for a room?" the man asked.

"Nope. A man and wife. They just got married, I un-derstand."

"Who're you?"

Longarm showed the man his badge. Leaning the broom against the wall beside him, the fellow said, "The Bolts told me you might be coming after them."

"Good. I'd like to see them."

"They're gone."

"Where?" Longarm asked.

"That's for me to know and you to find out, Marshal."

"You're aiding and abetting escaped fugitives."

"Them ain't fugitives, and you know it."

"You are not helping either of them by not telling me."

"That's for me to judge."

Longarm knew he could not threaten the man, and he was in no frame of mind to try. Jane-Marie and Bolt, now that they were newlyweds, it seemed, were on the side of the angels. And Longarm was the big bad wolf come to blow their house down.

Without thanking the man, he turned and left.

A trip to the livery stable and the stagecoach office was fruitless. The word was out, evidently: tell this lawman nothing. It was dark by the time he got back to the hotel. Rosemary was waiting for him in a dusty armchair in the hotel lobby. She got up as he entered.

"Are they here?"

"I'm not sure. The whole town is protecting them. No one will tell me anything."

"All the world loves a lover," she sneered.

"I am beginning to realize that."

"See that man over there?" Rosemary was indicating a short, bluff fellow with white hair and a scarlet face who was sitting in an easy chair on the other side of the lobby.

135

He had a cigar stuck in the corner of his mouth and was reading a paper.

"I see him."

"He works at the express office," she said.

"That so?"

"Maybe a few drinks and the company of an exciting woman will make him cooperate some."

Longarm nodded. "All right. See what you can find out."

Rosemary left him and moved across the lobby. Longarm looked the other way and did not glance back until Rosemary and the express clerk were leaving the hotel lobby together, heading for the saloon next door.

Longarm got his key from the desk clerk and went up to his room.

He was awakened from a sound sleep by a knock on his door. He sat up and glanced out the window. Outside it was pitch black: well past midnight.

"Longarm!" Rosemary whispered fiercely through the door. "It's me."

He threw back the covers, padded across the floor, and opened the door. Rosemary ducked quickly into his room. Still dressed, she smelled of cigar smoke and beer.

"I'm sorry," she said. "I can't stay."

He shrugged. "What did you find out?"

"Jane-Marie and Bolt left on the stage this morning."

"Where to?"

"Silver City. Now get your beauty sleep. I've got to pay the man for that precious bit of information."

"We'll take the stage out tomorrow, first thing."

Moving out through the open doorway, she glanced back at him. "We will if I can get ready in time. This is going to be a long night."

"Be good."

"I'm always good."

Chuckling, Longarm closed the door and went back to bed.

They reached Silver City at dusk two days later. An hour before they had passed through Blackwood, the mining town where he had freed Doc Hamlet from a lynch mob. While the stagecoach driver was picking up the mail and the other passengers took the opportunity to get out and stretch their legs, Longarm stayed in the coach and sat well back. There was no sense asking for trouble.

As soon as the stage pulled up in front of the Frontier Hotel, Longarm climbed out gratefully, stretched his tall frame, then carried Rosemary's luggage and his gear into the hotel and registered. This time they were in the same room. As Rosemary went upstairs ahead of him to settle in, Longarm showed the desk clerk his badge and asked to see the register. He ran his finger down the page slowly, but he saw no couples listed as having arrived the day before.

"I'm looking for a man and wife. I have reason to believe they came in on the stage from Iron Creek yesterday."

"That's impossible, Marshal. I was on the porch when the stage rolled in. Two drummers, a cattleman, and a local businessman got out. There was no couple."

"You sure of that?"

"Positive."

"Thank you."

Longarm left the lobby and walked across the street to the stagecoach office.

The express clerk, wearing a green eyeshade, was sitting behind a window on a high stool. He put down his pen when Longarm entered.

"Who was the jehu on that run from Iron Creek yesterday?"

137

"That'd be Mike Dillon."

"Where can I find him?"

"He's in back," the clerk said, gesturing over his shoulder with his pen. "Asleep."

"I'd like to go in and talk to him."

"Sure. Go right ahead. He should be sober by now."

Longarm walked past the clerk, pushed through a door, and found himself in a small, stuffy room with cots against the wall. On one cot lay a large, dark-haired fellow with black, beetling brows. As Longarm got closer to the jehu, he caught a whiff of raw whiskey.

The jehu groaned slightly as Longarm shook him. His eyes flickered open. He moistened dry lips. "What's the matter, bub?"

"You had two passengers on your run yesterday. Newlyweds. You picked them up at Iron Creek."

The driver sat up carefully. Peering at Longarm through painful slits, he nodded. "I remember."

"Good. How come they didn't get here?"

"They left the stage."

"*Left* it? What do you mean?"

"Just what I said."

"Where?"

"At the Black Canyon way-station."

Longarm remembered the station. The driver of his stage had picked up a fresh team there and the passengers had been allowed to stretch their limbs and relieve themselves. There was food, too, for those who wanted it. It was a good thirty miles south of Silver City.

Longarm swore softly, thanked the jehu, and left.

He was crossing back to the hotel when a burly miner stepped off the boardwalk and blocked his path. Behind him, two other miners drew up as well, their grimy faces set, their eyes boring into Longarm's. The miner blocking his path seemed vaguely familiar, but Longarm was having difficulty placing the man.

"Well, well, well," said the miner. "Look who it is, sure enough."

"That's the son of a bitch, all right," said one of the other two men standing behind him.

The third fellow just grunted.

"There must be some mistake," Longarm said easily, though he was uneasily aware that there might not be.

"There ain't no mistake, mister," said the burly miner. "Where's that hoss-thievin' Indian? And that other bastard?"

Longarm remembered then. These were the miners from Blackwood, part of the mob that had tried to prevent Longarm from rescuing Doc Hamlet. And this burly miner standing in front of him was the same fellow Old Buffalo had ridden past and plucked off the ground, preventing him from getting off his shot at Longarm.

"Where's that bastard?" the miner demanded. "Where's Doc Hamlet?"

"I don't know."

"You let the son of a bitch loose."

"He rode off after we took him."

"I knew you weren't no peace officer. You let him go so he could poison more innocent people. That it?"

"If you men had been willing to give him a fair trial, there'd have been no need for me to step in. Mob justice is not justice."

"Save the bullshit, mister."

The three men closed swiftly about him. The miner's right arm moved slightly and Longarm felt the hard muzzle of a Colt pressing urgently into his stomach just above his belt. At the same time, the other two men lifted their weapons from their holsters. It was completely dark by this time, and there were few on the sidewalk who took notice of the

139

four men clustered in the street by the boardwalk. Those who did suspect something looked quickly away and hurried on down the street, anxious to put distance between themselves and trouble.

"What'll we do now, Hank?" one of the men asked the burly miner.

"We got ourselves a hanging coming. We string him up."

"Not here," said the third one nervously.

"Of course not," replied Hank.

"Then where?"

"Hangman's Gulch."

"Yeah," said the second one. "That'd be perfect."

With his left hand Hank pushed aside the skirt to Longarm's frock coat and lifted his Colt out of its holster. Slipping the Colt into his belt, Hank stepped back and waggled his revolver at Longarm.

"Turn around, lawman," he said. "Easy, like."

Longarm turned.

"You see them three horses in front of the saloon?" Hank asked. "Walk over and mount that gray. Don't make no sudden moves, or we'll shoot you down in the street here."

Longarm did not for a moment doubt their resolve. He crossed the street and mounted the horse. Hank climbed up behind him, grabbed the reins, and led the other two horsemen down the main street at an easy canter. Few townsmen gave the four riders a glance.

A mile or so from town, Hank turned the gray off the road toward a dark cluster of hills. Before long a canyon opened up before them. They halted, and Hank and his two companions dismounted.

"Get down, lawman," Hank said.

Longarm stepped off the horse.

Hank pointed to a tree on the rim of the canyon. In the moon's cold wash it stood out pale and leafless. It had evidently been struck some time ago by a bolt of lightning. One single heavy branch extended out over the canyon, making it a perfect hangman's tree and the gorge below it Hangman's Gulch.

Hank walked over to the tree and flung a hangman's noose over the limb. Catching it as it came down, he turned back to Longarm, a grim smile on his face. "You done cheated us out of one hanging, lawman. This one, you won't have a thing to say about."

"Think it over, Hank," Longarm told him.

"Why in hell should I?"

"This'll make you no better than Doc Hamlet."

"You think so? Them who died from Doc Hamlet's poison died slow, lawman. Real slow."

"We could hear their screams," said the second miner.

"That's right," said the other one. "This'll be a lot quicker. It's a cryin' shame we ain't got any of Doc Hamlet's Golden Medical Discovery for you."

"Tie his hands behind him," said Hank, "and push him over here."

"We gonna use a horse?"

"We don't need it. He's just going to take a long step down."

"Don't do this, Hank," Longarm said.

"Shut up."

Longarm felt the second miner grab his left wrist and pull it around behind him. The third miner caught sight of Longarm's watch chain.

"Hey!" he said, reaching for it. "Look here! A watch."

Longarm pushed back.

"Take it easy," he said. "You'll break it. I'll give it to you."

Longarm lifted the watch out gently, then the fob. In the darkness not one of the men caught the glint of the derringer's barrel. Spinning away suddenly, Longarm went down on one knee, cocking and aiming the weapon in one quick movement.

"He's got a gun!" cried the nearest miner.

Before the man could bring up his gun, Longarm fired point-blank into his face. With a scream he went reeling back. For an instant he teetered on the rim of the gorge, then he toppled from sight. The second miner was reaching back for his own weapon when Longarm clubbed him with the butt of his derringer. As the man staggered back before Longarm, Hank fired. The slug plowed into the miner's back, slamming him forward onto Longarm.

As Longarm went down, he saw Hank rushing up to finish him. Longarm aimed at Hank and fired point-blank. The round smashed into his chest. Hank gasped, dropped his gun, and staggered back. As he sagged to the ground, Longarm flung aside the miner Hank had wounded and hurried over to him. Yanking his Colt from Hank's belt, he cocked it and stepped back. Hank lifted his head and glared at Longarm.

"Go ahead, you son of a bitch. Shoot me."

"I ought to."

"Do it!"

With a sigh Longarm holstered his Colt, then knelt beside the man to examine his wound. It did not look good. Hank would need medical attention. Longarm pulled the miner to his feet, then flung him over his shoulder and carried him over to the gray.

"Hang on," Longarm said as he helped him into his saddle. "I'm taking you back to Silver City."

"What about Abe?"

"He the one you shot?"

"Yeah."

"I'll go see."

142

Longarm walked over to the wounded miner. He was sprawled face down and lying very still. Longarm turned him over. Abe stared with sightless eyes up at Longarm.

"Dead," Longarm told Hank.

Without a word Hank dug his heels into the gray's flanks and bolted away into the darkness. Longarm stood up and listened as the sound of the horse's pounding hooves gradually faded.

With a fatalistic shrug, he bent and flung the dead man over one of the horses, tied him on securely, then mounted the remaining horse and started back to Silver City.

By the time Longarm had finished delivering the miner's body, there was a growing crowd outside the undertaker's establishment.

"Was that Abe you just brought in, mister?" a miner standing close asked.

"Reckon so."

"You kill him?"

"Nope. A friend of his did. It was a mistake."

"What's that?"

"His friend was aiming at me."

"I know you," someone else cried. "You're that lawman let Doc Hamlet free!"

"That's right. I'm a lawman. Stand back and let me through."

As Longarm strode toward them, they stepped aside reluctantly. He kept going through the slowly parting crowd, entered the hotel, and went up to his room.

She was in bed waiting for him. She smiled sleepily. "What did you find out?"

"The newlyweds left the stage at the Black Canyon way-station. I figure they must have bought horses there and headed west."

143

Rosemary sighed. "Such fools! Now come here. I've been waiting."

Longarm stopped beside the bed and looked down at her. She was not bothering to cover her breasts as she lay there looking up at him. With a sudden, mischievous smile, she raised her arms to him. Ignoring the invitation, he sat down beside her on the bed.

"We've got to move out," he told her. "Now."

"Longarm! Right this minute? Why?"

He told her about the three miners who had just tried to hang him and the angry, belligerent crowd he had just pushed through downstairs.

She sat up when he had finished, her dark, lustrous hair cascading down over her ivory breasts. "But aren't we safe in this hotel?"

He left the bed and went to the window and looked out. The crowd of miners was growing. He could hear a few angry shouts. "No," he told her.

"So what do we do?"

"Do you insist on going with me?"

"We've come this far. Yes."

"Maybe you're right at that. That crowd down there sounds pretty damn ugly—and it didn't take long for them to gather."

"That settles it. I'm coming with you."

"Get dressed and pack your gear. Leave most of your stuff with the hotel. We'll have to travel light. I'll rent two mounts and come back for you."

"Where are we going?"

"The Black Canyon way-station."

Rosemary flung aside the bedcovers and stood up. Longarm contemplated her nakedness and felt a raw stirring in his groin. But that would have to wait, he told himself. Maybe on the ride south they could find a spot and rest up.

144

The thought quickened him. He picked up his bedroll and rifle and started for the door.

"I'll be right back," he told her, pulling open the door. "Be ready."

The owner of the livery stable did not want to rent Longarm two horses until he saw Longarm's badge. Then, and reluctantly, he allowed Longarm to choose two mounts. Longarm took a big black for himself and a bay for Rosemary. Keeping to the back alleys, he took a long, circuitous route to the rear of the hotel and tethered the mounts to its rear porch. Entering the hotel, he hurried up the back stairs to their room.

It was empty.

The large suitcase Rosemary was leaving at the hotel was packed and waiting in the middle of the floor. But Rosemary apparently had already left. Assuming she was waiting for him downstairs in the lobby, he grabbed her luggage and carried it downstairs.

The desk clerk blinked the sleep out of his eyes as Longarm approached the front desk. "Leaving, Mr. Long?"

Longarm nodded.

"At this hour?"

"That's a noisy crowd you got out there."

"Ah, yes. But, from what I hear, you're the one they're so angry about."

Without bothering to reply, Longram asked, "Where's the girl?"

"Your . . . companion?"

"That's right. This is her luggage. We'll be back for it or we'll send for it."

"Of course. But I'm afraid I have no idea where the girl is, Mr. Long."

"You mean she's not down here?"

He looked quickly about the lobby and then back at Longarm. "As you can see, she's not here. And she has not come down. I would have seen her."

Longarm slapped Rosemary's luggage up onto the desk and hurried back upstairs to the room.

"Rosemary," he called softly, feeling foolish.

There was no response. Longarm hurried down the back stairs and out to the waiting horses. She was not there either.

Where the hell was she?

Chapter 12

Standing there uncertain on the back porch, Longarm heard the mob storm into the hotel lobby. At the same time he saw three or four liquored-up miners carrying torches into the alley farther down. He flung himself onto the black and gave the animal its head, charging down the alley until he reached the edge of town. Cutting south, he glanced back. A few riders were coming after him, but they were not coming hard enough, and before long they had been swallowed up in the darkness.

Longarm rode until well past midnight, then made a dry camp. Off at dawn, he arrived at the way-station late that same day.

As he rode up to the hitch rack in front of the station, the stationmaster stepped out onto the low porch. His black floppy-brimmed hat was in one hand and he was mopping his face with the other. He was a squat, broad-beamed man with powerful arms and a seamed round face. His mustache was gray, as was his hair, and behind him in the doorway appeared his wife, a stout, pleasant-looking woman.

"Howdy, mister," the stationmaster said. "Light and set a spell."

"Name's Custis Long," said Longarm, swinging down and dropping his reins over the hitch rail. "Much obliged."

"Angus McCloud," the stationmaster replied, shaking Longarm's hand. "And this here's my wife, Anna."

Anna nodded quickly, obviously pleased at this break in their lonely routine, and vanished inside to put on the coffee.

Longarm stepped into the log building, McCloud following in after him. There were four large deal tables and chairs filling most of the long room. These were evidently set aside for the stagecoach passengers. McCloud's wife had scrubbed the table spotless and the places were already set.

Off to the right near a huge black wood stove was a smaller table and four chairs. Toward this table McCloud led Longarm.

"You just settle in right here," he told Longarm, "and I'll see to your horse."

"I'd appreciate that. He's been driven hard."

"I could tell that."

As soon as McCloud was gone, his wife placed a gleaming cup and saucer down in front of him. It was obvious she welcomed this opportunity to speak to Longarm alone.

"You're after them two, ain't you?" she said softly.

"Which two?"

"Them two what dropped off the stage to Silver City. Mr. and Mrs. Bolt."

"How did you know I was after them?"

"Mrs. Bolt described you to me," she said, going back to the stove for the pot of coffee. "I guess you might say I expected you."

"How so?"

"Because that was what Mrs. Bolt wanted."

"What do you mean by that?"

Mrs. McCloud poured his coffee. "She was not happy, poor girl. She told me if you came looking for her to be sure and tell you which way she was going."

Longarm smiled grimly to himself. Already what he had predicted was happening. The farther Jane-Marie got from England, the faster she was unwinding.

"Of course I didn't tell Angus," Mrs. McCloud went on. "He thought they made such a perfect couple."

"How come Jane-Marie confided in you?"

The woman chuckled. "I understood perfectly. The same thing happened to me. She loves her husband too much to go against his wishes—even though his eagerness to get to Oregon seems foolish to her."

Longarm smiled. "You mean that's what happened to you?"

She nodded. "Something like it. You don't think living out here in the middle of nowhere is the fulfillment of all my youthful dreams, do you?"

"No, I reckon not. And you say you could tell Jane-Marie felt that way, too?"

The woman smiled and nodded emphatically. "You might say I recognized the symptoms. Besides, that woman's got better sense."

"That's what I thought, until she ran off with Bolt."

McCloud returned. His wife broke off, poured her husband's coffee, then brought a cup and saucer over for herself and joined them.

"That black's done in," McCloud told Longarm.

"You got a mount I can take?"

"Where'd you get this one?"

"The livery stable in Silver City."

"I'll let you take your pick of what I got outside in the

barn. I can take the black on in to Silver City when I go in for more horseflesh."

"Done."

"That mean you'll be riding out soon?"

"It does," Longarm replied.

McCloud's wife spoke up then. "He's after the Bolts."

McCloud frowned. "That so, Long?"

Longarm nodded.

"What they done?"

"It ain't that. It's what I don't want them to do."

McCloud chuckled. "Well, I ain't gonna say I'm surprised. I could tell they was runnin' from something, they was in such a blamed hurry to move out."

"Which way did they go?"

"Northwest, through Pine Cliff Pass. They're on their way to Oregon through the South Pass. I told them they should've stayed on the stage to Silver City. That would've put them a good thirty miles closer to it."

Longarm finished his coffee and stood up. "I'll be moving on, then."

As he left the cabin with McCloud, he touched the brim of his hat to Anna McCloud. "Much obliged, ma'am."

"Good luck, Mr. Long. I hope you find them two safe and sound."

"So do I."

As Longarm selected a big, powerful chestnut, McCloud cleared his throat. "Didn't want to say anything to you in front of the wife, Long—but I been hearin' things about a renegade band of Sioux hereabouts."

"You mind spellin' that out, McCloud?"

"I was out in the back pasture when some troopers came by searching for them."

"When was this?"

"A couple of days ago. I told the lieutenant I ain't seen

150

any Sioux and he rode off. Just thought I'd warn you. You know how crazy them bucks got once they break out of an agency."

"I'll keep an eye out. Much obliged."

Longarm tightened the cinch straps, then led the chestnut from the barn. McCloud kept pace with him.

"Sure is lonely country here, Long. And word of them Sioux don't make it any less so. Sometimes I wonder why I ever did leave Ohio for this wild, Godforsaken country."

Stepping into the saddle, Longarm looked down at McCloud. "Then why did you?"

"My wife. Why, Anna was plumb crazy for us to come out here and make a clean start for both of us. I didn't want to disappoint her."

As Longarm swung the chestnut around, he looked back at the stationmaster. "I suggest you go in and talk to her *now,* McCloud."

Longarm watched the man frown, then turn and move back to the cabin. Smiling to himself, Longarm clapped spurs to the chestnut and headed out.

Beyond the pass two days later, early in the morning, Longarm caught the dim tracery of smoke lifting above a morning campfire. It was coming from well beyond the next ridge. Cresting the ridge about fifteen minutes later, he pulled up and studied the high timbered slopes and parkland that stretched before him clear to the horizon.

He was about to push on across the ridge when he caught the glint of sunlight on metal in the timber covering a distant slope. Keeping his eye on the spot, he waited patiently until the quick flash came a second time. A moment later two riders cut across a small clearing and vanished into the timber beyond.

That single glimpse had been enough.

Longarm recognized one of the riders immediately. Rose-mary. Who was with her he had no idea. But now he knew where she had vanished to, and why. Rosemary was after Jane-Marie, hoping to accomplish what she had set out to do so long before—eliminate the one remaining obstacle to that title she wanted so badly.

It was still light when Longarm found cover in the timber above Rosemary's camp. She and her male companion had found a small clearing close beside a stream. The campfire was blazing and Longarm could see the two figures huddled over it. The odor of hot coffee found its way up the slope to where he crouched—coffee and beans. With both hands, Rosemary set the coffeepot carefully down onto the fire's dying coals, then leaned closer to the fire. Longarm didn't blame her. It would be dark soon, and already the mountain night was cool.

The man with Rosemary finished eating and lay down near the fire, apparently worn out. His back was to Longarm and Longarm could hear his dim drone as he spoke to Rose-mary. There was something oddly familiar about his voice, but try though he might, Longarm could not place it. After a while, Rosemary lay down also beside her companion. There was no fooling around between them, however, which—considering Rosemary's amorous proclivities—surprised Longarm.

Stirring himself, Longarm cat-footed it down the slope and across the clearing toward their campsite, counting on the sound of the fast-running mountain stream to drown out his approach. Gun drawn, he leaned over Rosemary and saw the rawhide wound about her wrists. At that instant, her companion rolled over and shoved the muzzle of his already cocked sixgun up into Longarm's face.

Jim Blade had not died of cholera after all.

152

Blade smiled coldly. "Thought you'd take the bait. Now drop that iron or I'll blow a hole in your face big enough to ride a stagecoach through."

Longarm tossed his Colt a few feet away and straightened up. Blade stood up, his sixgun still trained on Longarm. He had not been resting, Longarm realized ruefully. He had been waiting.

"Yes, sir," Blade said cheerfully. "Soon's I caught sight of you yesterday I knew what it would take to snare you."

"I'm sorry, Longarm," Rosemary said miserably. "He would have killed me if I tried to warn you."

"Forget it."

Longarm turned his attention back to Jim Blade. The last time he had seen the man, he had appeared to be dying from the cholera. From the look of him now, it looked as if he *had* died—and then been resurrected, like Lazarus. Blade had no more heft to him than a scarecrow. His clothes hung loosely on his frame, his face was sunken, and mad, haunted eyes peered out at Longarm from within deep hollows.

"I see you made it," said Longarm.

"No thanks to you, you son of a bitch."

"What about your brother?"

"Tommy's dead. He puked his guts out while I watched."

"Sorry to hear that."

"Sure you are."

"Put down that gun and talk sense, Blade."

"I'll put it down," he said, "after I take care of you. I've been waiting a long time."

"That'd be cold-blooded murder, Blade."

"He'll do it, Longarm!" Rosemary cried. "He's the one got them miners all riled up. Now he wants to kill us both for leaving him and Tommy."

"Blade, we had no choice," Longarm told him. "We had to leave you and your brother. You know that."

"Shit! You didn't have to leave us like that."

"I had no choice."

"Jane-Marie warned you about that cabin," Rosemary said. "But you wouldn't listen! You laughed at her. We didn't kill your brother. You did!"

Blade strode swiftly to Rosemary and kicked her viciously in the side. She grunted and went sprawling across the campfire, sending the coffeepot flying. The embers blazed up momentarily. With a tiny scream, Rosemary rolled free of the campfire and began beating clumsily with her bound hands at her smoking dress.

It was the only diversion Longarm was likely to get.

He flung himself through the air, catching Blade in the side. It was as if he had struck a rotted tree. Blade bent, then broke under his assault, crashing to the ground beneath him. But before Longarm could pin Blade beneath him, Blade lashed out with his gun, slamming Longarm on the side of his head.

The blow was a nasty one, and it slowed Longarm considerably.

He reached out for Blade and tried to wrest the gun from him. The gun discharged, the detonation so close to Longarm's ear it deafened him. A second time Longarm charged Blade, but it was like trying to capture smoke. Blade ducked aside and scrambled to his feet, still holding his gun.

Longarm looked up at Blade. The man was aiming carefully down at him, his eyes alight with madness.

"No!" Rosemary screamed.

She flung herself at Blade. He ducked easily, then swiped at her with his Colt. Longarm heard the heavy weapon slam into her skull. Rosemary sagged unconscious to the ground.

By then Longarm had managed to draw his derringer.

"Not this time, you son of a bitch!" Blade cried, kicking the weapon out of Longarm's hand.

Blade stepped back, crouched, and brought up his Colt again. He was panting with eagerness—and so anxious was he not to miss, he steadied his gun hand with his left.

A rifle cracked from the timber.

As Jim Blade crumpled to the ground, Old Buffalo broke from the timber and rode across the clearing toward the campfire. The Indian was wearing his derby hat and checked vest, with his huge bowie knife still stuck in the red sash around his waist.

And out from the timber behind him came a band of less flamboyantly dressed Sioux braves, six in all.

Retrieving his Colt and derringer, Longarm hurried over to Rosemary. She was not dead, just groggy from the blow. He shook her gently. She opened her eyes.

"How do you feel?" he asked.

"Awful. My head hurts."

"Can you get up?"

"I think so."

Longarm cut the rawhide binding Rosemary's wrists and helped her to her feet. Then he waited as Old Buffalo dismounted and approached them. The Indian nodded to them almost casually, as if coming upon them like this was perfectly normal. Then he looked down at the dead Jim Blade.

"He not die of white man's sickness, huh?"

"Guess not, Old Buffalo. Looks like he was destined to die of lead poisoning instead."

The Indian grunted and gazed shrewdly at Longarm. "You look for Bolt and his woman?"

Longarm nodded.

"That good." The old Sioux shook his head. "Sometimes white friends like fleas on old dog. Too close they stay, I think."

"You know where they are?"

"Horse woman ride, him break leg. So Bolt and his

woman double they ride on his horse. Pretty soon both walk. My braves come tell me. I watch them too and soon foolish Old Buffalo take pity. With my people now they stay. When my braves see you and tell me, glad am I you come. Now you take them away, back to white man's world. They no like, I think, world of Old Buffalo."

"I had an idea they'd be feeling this way by now."

"Good. Old Buffalo must take his people far from here."

"And where might that be?"

"Home to die Old Sioux medicine chief come from Canada. Say he before he die many buffalo in Canada. British Queen like Sioux. Let them hunt buffalo like old times. We go see if he lie or not."

"I hope he didn't," Longarm said.

"You get now your horse and ride to my camp."

Longarm nodded and hurried back up the slope to get his mount.

It was completely dark by the time they arrived at Old Buffalo's encampment. Longarm counted about sixteen lodges, but in the moonless night he could not be absolutely certain. Over to a lodge at the edge of the camp Old Buffalo led them. The lodge seemed situated in a spot lower and damper than the rest of the campground. It was obviously not a chief's lodge.

Longarm and Rosemary dismounted just as Jane-Marie threw back the entrance flap to the lodge.

With a squeal of delight, Jane-Marie flung herself into Rosemary's arms. So pleased was Jane-Marie to see a familiar face that she forgot all about Rosemary's treacherous hostility. And even Rosemary seemed glad to find her erstwhile friend safe and sound.

Bolt appeared in the lodge entrance. He nodded glumly to Longarm. "Glad to see you, Longarm."

"Are you?"

Bolt nodded as he glanced around him at the dark lodges. "Yes, I guess I really am, at that. This settlement is a far cry from the amenities of western civilization. My God, I don't think these aborigines *ever* bathe."

"Thought you would've known that."

"I knew it, but I didn't know it, if you know what I mean."

"I think maybe I do."

"And this wild, unpredictable land is no place for Jane-Marie. I can see that now."

"Even though you have each other?"

"Yes." He smiled ruefully at Longarm. "I must have sounded like such a bloody fool back there."

"You did. But there's an excuse for it."

"An excuse?"

"You were in love."

"And we still are," said Jane-Marie, leaving Rosemary to take her husband's arm. "But I do agree with him—and he with me. I have decided to return to Leadville. I did not kill Bill Barnstable. And I am hopeful that my innocence can be proven."

"And no matter what the outcome," said Bolt, "Jane-Marie knows I will stand by her."

The old Sioux chieftain had dismounted and was standing with quiet dignity to one side. Longarm turned to him. "Could you lend these pilgrims here fresh horses?"

"When they go?"

"First thing in the morning."

"That good. I give you tomorrow fine Indian ponies. Gift of Old Buffalo. His Sioux move out too."

The old chief turned and disappeared into the night. Longarm looked over at Rosemary. It was difficult to be sure of much in the dark, but it seemed to him that she looked confused, even subdued. It was dawning on her, maybe, that if events in Leadville went against Jane-Marie and gave Rosemary the opportunity to take from her the title she had fought so hard for, it would not be the triumph she had expected.

Not entirely.

"Come inside," said Jane-Marie to both of them. "This tipi is large enough for four—and if you can ignore the smell, maybe you'll be able to get some sleep."

Rosemary looked unhappily over at Longarm. Longarm shrugged. Rosemary ducked her head and entered the lodge, Longarm following after her. It was clear at once to both of them that Jane-Marie had not exaggerated, but by that time they were both too exhausted to care.

By mid-morning Jane-Marie and Bolt settled on two fine Sioux war ponies and Old Buffalo gave the order to break camp. As they rode out, Rosemary kept alongside Longarm, while Bolt and Jane-Marie rode behind them.

Once the excitement of seeing each other again had worn off, the two women became once again cold, aloof enemies—as if a certain visible only to them had slammed down between them. Longarm always found it difficult to understand women. And this sudden about-face only confirmed the impossibilty of ever doing so.

Early the next day they reached Pine Tree Pass, their Sioux escort still with them. Old Buffalo had told Longarm he would stay with them until they made it through the pass. He wanted to make sure that Bolt and Jane-Marie did not wear out their Sioux war ponies as they had the horses they had purchased at the way-station.

Longarm glanced back. A long, ragged line of warriors and their women and children—some on horseback, some walking beside their packhorses—trailed over the thinly wooded high country behind them, Old Buffalo at their head. As Longarm watched, a scout who had been riding ahead crested a slope and galloped toward the chief.

It was clear at once from the way the Indian rode that he was not bringing good news.

Turning his mount, Longarm told Rosemary and the others to keep going, then galloped to Old Buffalo. As he pulled his mount to a halt beside Old Buffalo, the scout was already speaking rapidly to the chief, but Longarm was able to pick up most of it. A mile beyond the next timbered foothill a column of troopers was riding straight toward them. At their present course the bluecoats would intercept the Sioux.

"Have the troopers seen us yet?" Longarm asked Old Buffalo.

"No. Little Fox say they do not know we are here."

"Good."

"Why you say good?"

"I have a plan."

"Speak."

"You and your people move into the timber on the slopes above us. Bolt and I will swing around and approach the troopers from the south. We'll tell them we saw you and your people heading southwest, toward the way-station. As soon as they turn to intercept you, you and your people can move north to Canada."

"It is good plan."

"Don't waste any time. Head up into that timber now."

Nodding briskly, Old Buffalo spoke sharply to the braves who had ridden up beside them. The warriors broke back and began issuing orders. The entire column of Indians turned and began hurrying up the slope toward the timber.

"This is goodbye, Old Buffalo," Longarm said.

Old Buffalo shook his head. "Maybe not this time goodbye it is. Soon my people hunt buffalo again—and maybe you will join me."

"I'll think about it, Old Buffalo. Give my regards to the Queen."

The Sioux chief wheeled his mount and started after his people. This time, watching him go, Longarm knew what the wily old chieftain had meant earlier when he had rattled on about hearing the voices of his people calling to him in the wind and the tall grass of the hills. The only place left for Old Buffalo and his people now was Canada, and getting there would not be easy. But if any chief could pull it off, Old Buffalo was that man.

He was no agency Indian, and that was a fact.

By this time Bolt had ridden back to join him. Pointing to the Indians hurrying into the timber, he asked, "What in the bloody hell's going on, Longarm?"

"There's a cavalry patrol on its way. And it looks like you and I are going to be doing some play-acting."

"Would you care to explain that?"

Longarm did and when he had finished, he asked, "You willing to go along?"

"Of course."

"Okay. Go tell the others what I just told you."

Before long the four riders were riding south at a brisk trot. Half an hour later, having circled and cut due north again, Longarm sighted the troopers ahead of him. They were moving directly across his path. At sight of Longarm and the others, the column halted. A moment later the lieutenant in charge left his command and galloped through the tall grass toward them, his sergeant following at a respectful distance.

Longarm and Bolt told the women to stay back, then rode out to meet the lieutenant.

The lieutenant pulled to a halt before Longarm. "What

are you people doing out here?"

The lieutenant was a fine horseman, Longarm noted. He could not have been more than twenty-two or -three, and he looked to be fresh out of West Point. Despite his youth, he appeared quite confident and sure of himself.

"We've been looking for you," Longarm replied.

"Oh?"

"We've sighted a large body of Sioux heading toward the way-station southwest of here."

"The station at Black Canyon?"

"Yes."

"How long ago?"

"Less than an hour."

"How'd you know where to find us?"

"We saw you headin' for the pass earlier, when we were heading south. Guess maybe you didn't see us."

"And so you rode north to find us again."

"That's right, lieutenant."

"The women, too."

"We didn't want to leave them alone that close to so many Indians," said Bolt.

The sergeant, a thin blade of a man, nudged his mount closer. "You sure they're Sioux?"

"They're Sioux, all right."

"A war party?"

"No. They had their women and children and old folks with them. It looked like close to ten or fifteen lodges, all told."

"Thank you, mister," said the lieutenant. "And what would your name be?"

"Long, sir. Custis Long."

"I am much obliged, Mr. Long."

With that the lieutenant wheeled his horse and galloped back to his troopers, the sergeant with him.

161

Watching him go, Bolt said to Longarm, "I do believe we have no choice now but to get the hell out of here."

"You're right, Bolt. It's on to Leadville for us—and we'd better not look back."

Chapter 13

Three days later, close to nightfall, they reached Leadville. After leaving their weary mounts at the livery, they registered at the Clarendon Hotel. Then Longarm left Bolt with Jane-Marie and Rosemary, and went looking for the sheriff.

He was crossing the street on the way to the sheriff's office when he glimpsed someone peering at him from the door of a saloon. Startled, Longarm halted and looked back. He thought he recognized the face, but it was so gaunt, so ravaged, Longarm could not be certain. As Longarm caught the man's eye, the fellow ducked hastily back into the saloon.

Swinging back onto the sidewalk, Longarm shouldered aside the batwings and strode into the saloon. Coils of cigar and pipe smoke hung so heavily in the air that Longarm had a difficult time making out individual faces. The saloon was so jammed that Longarm could push his way only slowly through the crowd to the bar. He kept going until he had gone the length of the saloon; then he pushed his way back toward the entrance.

By that time he had stared into so many grimy faces, he was pretty well convinced that it was only his overworked imagination that caused him to think he had seen who he thought he had. He had ridden a long way that day, and was close to exhaustion.

He left the saloon and crossed the street to the sheriff's office. It was located in a new, unpainted jailhouse. The sheriff was at his desk and got to his feet when Longarm entered. He was a tall, graying man, slow-talking and easygoing. His name was Ned Ballantine, and as soon as the two men finished introducing themselves, Ballantine pulled a bottle of whiskey and two shot glasses from his drawer and poured Longarm a drink.

As Longarm took the drink, he told the sheriff why he had just brought back to Leadville the woman he knew as Sarah Smith.

When Longarm had finished, the sheriff took a deep breath and sat back in his chair. "And you say her real name's Jane-Marie Darnsforth, and that she's not guilty of killing Bill Barnstable?"

"That's right."

"You understand, Long, this means I'm going to have to take her into custody. Where's she staying?"

"At the Clarendon. But I want your promise, Sheriff, that you'll give me all the help I need to clear her."

"What makes you think you can?"

"Jane-Marie told me what happened."

"She did, did she? And what was supposed to have happened?"

"Frankie Paige shot Bill Barnstable. It was a lovers' quarrel. Frankie thought Barnstable was paying too much attention to Jane-Marie."

164

The sheriff frowned and leaned back to listen further.

"The trouble was Jane-Marie saw Frankie shoot Barnstable—with her own pocket Smith and Wesson—so Frankie paid Doc Hamlet to get rid of the body for her and kidnap Jane-Marie. Later, Doc Hamlet was supposed to kill her."

"That's a pretty wild tale this here Sarah Smith told you."

"I believe it," Longarm said.

Ballantine shrugged. "You won't find many in town who will, Marshal. Frankie Paige is a pretty important person in this town. Her word carries weight, and I don't need to tell you, her testimony tells a different story. This here Sarah Smith stole some of Frankie's jewelry when she lit out, and when Barnstable went after her to get it back for Frankie, he ended up with a bullet in his gut."

"And that's all you got?"

"What do you mean?"

"Just Frankie Paige's word?"

"Hell, no. Frankie's girls told the same story."

"Well, it didn't happen that way, Ballantine. I say we go talk to a few more of Frankie's girls. I got a hunch they'll be telling a different story this time around."

Ballantine shrugged. "Even if they did, who'd believe them? Maybe you don't understand, Long. Frankie Paige is pretty well regarded in this town."

"Hell, Ballantine, she's just another madam."

"Maybe so, but she contributes a heap to the local charities, especially the fire department. A little while ago I heard they was even thinking of making her an honorary member."

"Which means she can get away with murder?"

"Now, I didn't say that."

"Then haul Frankie Paige in. Question her."

"Oh, hell, I can't do that. One of her best girls takes

special care of me. Why, I'm like a father to her. Let Frankie be."

"Then you won't help."

"Long, be reasonable. If all you've got is that girl's testimony, forget it. It would just be her word against Frankie's. And there ain't nobody in this town going to believe one of Frankie's ex-girls over Frankie herself. You'd just be raisin' a stink for no good reason."

"There is a reason. A damn good one. Jane-Marie wants to clear her name."

"All right. I'll deal. Leave Frankie alone and I'll give you and this girl a forty-eight-hour start out of town. And I won't tell Frankie or anyone else she's been back. She can return to wherever she came from. Now that's fair enough, ain't it?"

Longarm finished his drink and got to his feet. "I'll give it some thought. But I don't have to like it, and I don't."

The sheriff shrugged. "I can't do any better, Long. Let me know what you decide. I'll be coming after this here Sarah Smith unless I hear from you by tomorrow morning. Early."

"Much obliged, Sheriff," Longarm said, turning and striding from the office.

When Longarm got back to the hotel, Bolt and Jane-Marie were waiting for him on the hotel's porch.

Before he could tell them of the result of his visit to the sheriff's office, they told him that Rosemary had already bid them goodbye and left. She was taking the next train back to Denver.

"When's the train supposed to leave?" Longarm asked.

"About now," said Bolt.

At that moment the sound of a train whistle as the train pulled out came to them. Longarm turned and glimpsed a line of coaches snaking out through the railyard.

Longarm turned back to Jane-Marie and Bolt. "Let's hope she's given up the idea of becoming the next Duchess of Clyde."

"I certainly hope so," said Jane-Marie.

"I wouldn't bet on it," said Bolt.

"She told me to say goodbye to you, Custis," Jane-Marie said.

"Did she now?"

Longarm looked back for a moment at the disappearing train, frowning thoughtfully. He would like to have said goodbye to her. After all, Rosemary had undoubtedly saved his life back there when she had flung herself at Jim Blade. With a shrug he turned to Bolt and Jane-Marie.

"The sheriff has made us an offer," he told them, leading them over to a circle of wicker chairs in the corner of the veranda to gain privacy.

"An offer?" Jane-Marie asked eagerly.

"Yes, but I don't think you'll like it."

"Let's hear it," said Bolt.

"He's willing to give Jane-Marie time to clear out. He won't press charges."

"How much time?"

"Forty-eight hours. I'm to give him Jane-Marie's answer by morning."

"I don't understand," said Jane-Marie.

"He doesn't want to stir up trouble for Frankie Paige. He points out that it will be your word against hers. But I figure he's willing to accept the possibility that Barnstable's murder took place the way you said it did. So for that reason he's giving you this chance to clear out."

"With my tail between my legs—a murderess fleeing the scene of her crime."

"Yes."

"You're right, Longarm," she said bitterly. "I *don't* like it."

"What do *you* think, Longarm?" asked Bolt. "Should we take the offer?"

"You know how I feel about it. But this decision is up to Jane-Marie and you."

"If we took this sheriff's offer," Jane-Marie said, "what assurance would I have that this murder charge would not follow after me to England?"

"None," said Longarm. "You have no assurance at all. And I can just imagine what Ned Buntline or those idiots who publish the dime novels would do with this kind of a story once they get wind of it."

"Yes," said Jane-Marie, nodding unhappily. "Someday, when I would least expect it, I'd wake up to find it in all the papers, my exploits here in Leadville and . . . elsewhere. I would have to come back then to face the charges—but no matter what the outcome, I'd be thoroughly discredited."

"I say forget the sheriff's offer," Longarm told her. "We've come back to confront the charge. Now's the time to do so."

"But how can I clear myself?" Jane-Marie asked. "You just said it is Frankie Paige's word against mine."

"I am going to do what I can to scare up other witnesses. There must have been others in Frankie's house who knew the trouble she was having with Bill Barnstable. Maybe even another witness to the murder."

"No, Longarm," Jane-Marie said unhappily. "There isn't."

"You're sure of that?"

"I am positive. It was late. Very late. No one else saw what happened. Doc Hamlet didn't see it, either. All he saw was Barnstable's dead body when Frankie paid him to take it away."

"Hold it."

168

Jane-Marie frowned. "What's the matter, Longarm?"

"Have you seen Doc Hamlet lately? I mean, since you ran out on him in Blackwood?"

"No, I haven't."

"Well, I think I have—and not too long ago."

"Doc Hamlet?"

"Yes. Only I was not certain it was him."

"Longarm, he knows the truth!"

"Where is he?" Bolt asked, jumping to his feet. "If I can get my hands on him, he'll be squealing like a pig before I get through with him."

Longarm got to his feet also. "I don't know where he is now. But I got a pretty good idea where I might find him."

"Where?"

"Never mind that. I won't be long, I don't think. Stay here."

"If you say so, Longarm," said Bolt.

"I say so."

Longarm left the porch and cut up Harrison Avenue to West Fifth. When he reached Frankie Paige's parlor house, he found that despite the early hour, it was going full blast.

The piano was booming away in the parlor. Above it could be heard the hearty peal of men's laughter, the clink of glasses, and above all, the occasional shrill laughter of girls who had already had too much to drink. He ducked aside as a miner with no pants on lunged past him. The man was trying to overhaul a scantily-clad girl who could not have been more than fifteen. Longarm kept going until he entered the parlor.

A girl immediately left the piano and started for him, smiling as winsomely as she could manage. She looked desperately tired already and was just as desperate to hide the fact.

"No, thanks," Longarm told her as she sidled up beside

him. "I came in to see an old friend of mine—Doc Hamlet."

"Doc Hamlet?" the girl repeated. It was clear she had no idea who Doc Hamlet was.

Longarm nodded. "He told me he'd be in here."

"Doc's with Frankie," said another girl who had overheard Longarm. She was a long-necked redhead. Grinning, she said, "But I figure they don't want to be disturbed."

"That's all right," Longarm said as he brushed past the redhead. "He's expecting me."

Longarm still remembered the layout of the parlor house from his first visit. He turned down a thickly carpeted hallway and came to the door to Frankie's private apartment. Without knocking, he pushed it open.

Doc Hamlet was standing by Frankie's desk as Frankie, holding a huge roll in one hand, counted out a hefty pile of bills onto her blotter.

Doc Hamlet spun about as Longarm stepped into the apartment. Longarm closed the door behind him. It was obvious to Longarm what was going on. Doc Hamlet was now in the act of blackmailing Frankie Paige.

As Hamlet turned, he pulled a small Colt from his jacket pocket. "Don't try to stop me, Long!" he said.

Longarm was astonished at how poorly Doc Hamlet looked. It was no wonder Longarm had had difficulty recognizing him earlier. The Doc's eyes were bloodshot, his cheeks sunken, his skin as sallow and cracked as old parchment. Ravaged by fear, he seemed to be wasting away. And Longarm thought he knew why.

"What's the matter, Doc? You afraid them miners are going to catch up to you the way they did your black friend?"

Hamlet moistened dry lips. "They already came after Will Clay and strung him up. But they ain't goin' to catch me." He aimed the revolver at Longarm. "So don't you try to stop me."

"That's a pile of money you got there."

Swiftly, Hamlet reached down and snatched up the bills.

"How come, Frankie?" Longarm asked, looking at the madam. "What's this piece of offal got on you?"

"Murder," Hamlet sneered.

Longarm glanced back at Hamlet. "That makes you an accessory."

"Never mind that shit. Just get out of my way!"

Hamlet started for the door.

Ducking to one side, Longarm reached across his waist. The double-action .44 appeared in Longarm's right fist with such awesome speed that Hamlet paused in astonishment. But he was a desperate, foolish man.

He brought up his own weapon and cocked it.

With a scream of rage, Frankie Paige flung herself at Hamlet. The Doc was slammed sideways. He tried to catch himself. But when he struck the wall, he involuntarily squeezed off a shot. The bullet smashed into Frankie's chest, knocking her back behind the desk.

Dazed, Hamlet swung his revolver back to Longarm.

Longarm fired. The round slammed into Hamlet's shirt-front, stamping a neat hole in it. Hamlet staggered back but did not go down. As he tried to bring up his Colt again, Longarm strode closer and slammed the gun from his hand. As the revolver struck the wall, Hamlet sagged to the floor.

The door behind Longarm was flung open. Longarm turned to see the doorway fill instantly with frightened, wide-eyed faces. At sight of Frankie Paige slumped back into her chair, a large bloodstain spreading over her flowered dress, the horrified girls began screaming. Longarm blocked the doorway and pushed them back out into the hallway.

"Someone get the sheriff!" he told them. "And a doctor! Now!"

Chapter 14

In her small but sumptuously furnished bedroom, Frankie Paige lay face up on the scarlet silk coverlet of her bed. She was still wearing her print dress from the waist down, but from the waist up she was swathed in bandages. Standing at the foot of her bed was a white-haired Catholic priest, his prayer book held in clasped hands before him.

His examination finished, the doctor sat back in his chair. Glancing at the priest, he shook his head, then got to his feet. Though the doctor had successfully removed the bullet less than an hour ago, there was still massive internal bleeding, and there was evidently nothing further the doctor could do. The folds in the old priest's face grew deeper as he made the sign of the cross over Frankie.

Closing his bag, the doctor brushed past Longarm and left the room. Longarm stepped closer to the bed and looked down at the dying madam. The sheriff moved up beside him, and Longarm could hear the reporter from the local newspaper stepping closer as well.

Sitting down in the chair the doctor had vacated, Longarm leaned his face close to Frankie's. "Can you hear me, Frankie?" he asked gently.

She opened her eyes and turned her head a fraction. "I can hear you," she said, her voice low, but surprisingly vibrant.

"You don't have much time. Why don't you make a clean breast of it?"

She just looked up at him, her cold, glittering green eyes showing only contempt. But whether it was contempt for him or for death, he could not tell.

"Did you kill Big Bill Barnstable?" he asked.

"Yes," she said, glancing quickly at and then away from the priest. "Yes. I killed the son of a bitch, and I'll kill him again if we meet in Hell. He was making a play for that blonde tramp from England. He was throwing me over for her! He told me so himself, with a smile on his face."

"Who helped you dispose of the body?"

"Doc Hamlet."

Longarm glance at the reporter. "You got all that?"

For answer, the young man lifted his notepad so Longarm could see the writing on it.

"And the girl, Sarah Smith. She had nothing to do with Bill's murder?"

"I told you. It was me killed Bill. But I curse the day Sarah Smith came into my house!" Then she looked away from Longarm and stared up at the ceiling. "Now get out of here," Frankie rasped, her voice noticeably weaker. "All of you—except Father Riley."

Longarm led the way out of the room. Bolt and Jane-Marie were waiting for him in the narrow hallway. He told them quickly what Frankie had admitted to him and the other witnesses; then he turned to the sheriff.

Before he could say anything, the sheriff held up both

hands, indicating complete surrender. "You were right, Long. I heard her. And the whole town will read about it in the papers tomorrow. But I don't blame Frankie none for killing that no-account. Frankie took Bill in when he had nothing but the clothes on his back. She deserved better from him than she got."

"Maybe so," replied Bolt, "but she had no right to attempt to make Jane-Marie pay for her crime."

Jane-Marie spoke up then, her voice soft. "I peeked into the room, Custis. Poor Miss Paige looked so small, so pathetic, lying there. How awful." There were tears in her eyes.

"I reckon it's time we got out of here," said Bolt, taking Jane-Marie's arm.

"I agree," said Longarm.

Once outside the parlor house, Longarm pulled to a halt and looked at the sheriff. "Ned, you wouldn't happen to know a reasonably quiet place where a man could get wrap his tonsils around some real, honest-to-God Maryland rye, would you?"

"I know just the place," Ned replied with a grin, steering Longarm down the street. "Fact is, I could use a little of that myself."

Longarm waved good night to Jane-Marie and Bolt and told them not to wait up for him. Even though he had succeeded in clearing Jane-Marie, there were parts of this night he would just as soon forget.

Two weeks later, Longarm and Vail were waiting in the Denver train station to bid goodbye to the Duchess of Clyde and her husband, Alfred Bolt. It was a bright Sunday afternoon and the train for St. Louis was due at any moment. The four of them had been talking together quietly for the past fifteen minutes, the duchess with a restraint and show

175

of manners Longarm had not noticed before. It was as if at some moment between her arrival back in Denver a week ago and her appearance on this station platform today, she had looked in upon herself and concluded that she was indeed a duchess now and must assume all the manners and obligations that such a high station demanded.

". . . of course we will write," said Bolt, in answer to a jibe by Longarm.

"I'll hold you to that," Longarm told him.

"Don't worry," said Bolt. "I couldn't forget you easily, or that crazy Indian. And I will always be grateful for what you did for Jane-Marie and me."

"You were a help, yourself, Bolt," Longarm reminded him. "You and that rifle of yours."

"Alfred is quite correct," Jane-Marie broke in then. "You must never think I am ungrateful, Custis—or that I was the least bit insincere when I invited you to come stay with us in Dorsetshire. Really, you must come. I insist. I am sure you will be *quite* popular."

Longarm caught the hint of condescension in her tone, but said nothing. But Vail was under no such restraint. He stepped immediately closer, his jaw set, his expression suddenly combative.

"Well, now, Duchess," Vail drawled, "I don't think you'd better count on Longarm goin' that far. I plan to keep him pretty busy. We got a passel of gunslicks and other assorted females and madmen headin' west—most of 'em packin' iron and lookin' for an easy way to make a buck, and every one of 'em readin' the latest foolishness in Ned Buntline's dime novels. No, ma'am, Longarm won't have no time to go sashayin' off to Merry England—just so's you can show him off like some prize bull to your fine ladies and silk-hatted gents."

Jane-Marie was immediately aware of how angry the old

lawman was with her and how expertly he had put her in her place. Realizing her mistake, she stammered. "Well, certainly, Marshal Vail," she managed, blushing slightly. "If as you say, Marshal Long is going to be so very busy . . ."

"He is," Vail assured her.

"Yes. Well, indeed, I am certainly sorry to hear it."

"I'm not, Duchess," Longarm told her with a smile gentle enough to take the sting out of Vail's anger. "Billy here keeps me in the saddle, and that's the way I like it. Tea parties and lawn croquet ain't in my bag of tricks."

The train appeared then, sweeping around a bend in the tracks, its huge black snout swinging slowly toward the platform. Its thunderous approach silenced them and the four took an involuntary step back as the train's flared cowcatcher swept past them, the smokestack filling the air with a storm of tiny cinders and the acrid smell of burning anthracite.

Longarm ducked his face away and pulled the brim of his hat down to protect his face and eyes, as did the other three. For a moment the locomotive loomed enormously, powerfully above them. The pistoned wheels stroked by, and Longarm felt the savage furnace-flare of heat, after which came the heavy rolling rumble of the coach's wheels. A second later, they screeched in protest as they ground slowly to a halt.

Bolt turned to Longarm and Vail and shook their hands. Then he stepped back to allow Jane-Marie to bid her farewell. She extended a white-gloved hand to Longarm. He took it and held it for a moment, not quite sure what else to do with it, then let it drop. Turning to Vail, she allowed him the same privilege. He responded as Longarm had.

Then Jane-Marie took a slight step back and cleared her throat.

"Goodbye, Marshal Vail, Marshal Long," the Duchess

of Clyde said, her voice distant, as if she were looking down upon them from a great height. "I shall always be grateful for your help."

"Think nothing of it, Duchess," said Vail.

Longarm simply smiled and bowed.

Bolt took Jane-Marie's arm and escorted her toward their coach through the crowd of arriving and departing passengers. As the duchess was helped up into the train by the conductor a moment later, she turned one more time, found their faces in the crowd, and waved goodbye. Bolt waved also. Then they vanished into the coach.

The cab they picked up at the train station left them off at the Windsor Hotel. The two men entered and found a booth in the lounge. After ordering their drinks, Vail glanced across the table at Longarm, an amused gleam in his eye.

"Yes, sir, it sure as hell didn't take long for that little blonde heller to turn herself into a duchess."

Longarm laughed. "No, it didn't. Not long at all."

"And that's just the way the State Department wants it," Vail admitted. "Queen Victoria can't have ex-whores to tea, so more power to the new Duchess of Clyde. As far as this here federal district is concerned, the whole thing never happened."

"Suits me fine."

"Of course, if you hadn't cleared up that murder in Leadville, we wouldn't have been able to hush things up quite so neatly."

Their glasses and a bottle arrived. Longarm poured for both of them, took out a cheroot and passed one to Vail.

"I forgot to mention," Vail said, "Washington was pleased you got rid of that Blade gang while you was at it. They was gettin' to be a real nuisance. Wells Fargo was raisin' quite a stink."

Longarm lit his cheroot and leaned back, nodding. "I'm pleased if they are."

"By the way, you ever hear anything more from that other filly?"

"Rosemary Sutcliff?"

Vail nodded.

Longarm shook his head.

"That's funny," Vail mused.

"Why?"

"Wallace thinks he saw her in town a couple of days ago."

"Well, I ain't seen her."

"Maybe that's just as well. From what you told me, she's a real hell-raiser."

"She is that."

"There's just one more thing," Vail said, looking shrewdly at Longarm.

"What's that, chief?"

"I overheard Bolt mention something about an Indian. You didn't tell me about him."

"Nothin' much to tell."

"Well, it so happens we got a dodger on a renegade Sioux chief. He lit out from an agency south of here, and he wasn't very polite about it, either. Thing is, he was last seen in Leadville, getting on to a stage headin' for a town called Blackwood. Now, ain't that the same town where you had all that trouble with the miners?"

"That's the place, all right."

"Was it about this time you ran into that Indian?"

"Yep."

"Well, then. This here chief was a big, tough son of a bitch. He likes to wear a derby hat and a checked vest over his naked chest. He's got a round moon face. And he talks pretty good English, but he gets his words all twisted around."

179

"A real tough hombre, you said?"

"He sure is. He tore up three agency police gettin' away."

"Maybe he don't like livin' on a reservation."

"What the hell's that got to do with it?"

Longarm shrugged.

"Well?"

"Well, what?"

"You seen this here Indian?"

"What was his name?"

"Tall Buffalo."

Longarm smiled. "Vail, I never in all my life laid eyes on any Indian who called himself Tall Buffalo."

Vail stared hard at Longarm for a long moment. Then he reached for his drink. He knew Longarm was deliberately not answering him straight—but he also knew that if the lawman was holding out, he must have a damn good reason. After a moment longer, Vail took a deep breath and shrugged fatalistically.

"Oh, hell," he said, "what's one Sioux Indian chief, more or less? Soon enough they'll all be gone—like the buffalo."

Longarm said nothing. Vail was right. Almost. Maybe at that very moment somewhere in Canada Old Buffalo was sitting astride his paint, looking down at a grass-choked valley black with buffalo. Maybe. He hoped so.

A shadow fell over their booth. Longarm looked up. Rosemary was smiling down at him, dressed almost as she had been on the first day he had met her outside the hotel, when she was supposed to have been running from a masher.

Longarm smiled. "We were just talking about you," he said. "Won't you join us?"

"If you're sure I won't be intruding."

"As a matter of fact," said Vail, "there's work at the

office I have to catch up on. Sunday's the best day for that, I find." He slipped out of the booth. "See you Monday, Longarm. Be on time for a change, will you?"

He nodded goodbye to Rosemary and left.

Rosemary sat herself down carefully across from Longarm and arranged herself as prettily as she could. Longarm asked her what she wanted to drink, then ordered it for her. She was still a right smart-looking filly, he noted—her bold chin and sparkling blue eyes were very much in evidence. She seemed to have recovered her fortunes nicely. Longarm recalled what Jane-Marie had said once about her, that Rosemary always seemed to land on her feet—like a cat.

After Rosemary's drink came, she looked across at Longarm. "I just wanted to see you again, Custis."

"I'm glad you stopped by. I was sorry you left in such a hurry in Leadville."

"Really?"

"Yes, really. I would like to have had the chance to say goodbye."

She sighed miserably, then shook her head. "I am so ashamed. I did such terrible things. But you must believe me when I say it is all out of my system now—that fever to become the Duchess of Clyde. For a while it was all I could think of. I was willing to do almost anything to gain that title. I had been a poor country cousin all my life. The thought of gaining all that wealth, of attaining that position . . . I tell you, it drove me wild. Try to understand, Custis."

"I guess maybe I can," Longarm told her. "I've seen men caught up in gold fever. I suppose that's pretty close to the same thing."

She looked at him, eyes wide. "Oh, I'm so glad you understand."

181

He shrugged.

Sipping her drink, she looked across at him. "It was good between us, wasn't it, Custis?"

"Yes," he admitted. "We were good together."

"I have a room in this hotel," she told him softly. "It can be good for us again. I want to make amends, Custis."

He smiled and picked up his drink. "You don't have to."

"But I want to! You must let me."

"Why don't we have another drink first? It's early yet."

"Of course," she responded, pleased.

As soon as they entered her room, Rosemary closed the door with her back to Longarm, then turned to face him. There was a small pearl-handled derringer in her right hand.

"You kept me from that title!" she told him fiercely. "From all that wealth! I saved your life once—but I was a fool!"

"No, you weren't," Longarm told her as he started toward her. "Not at all. At that moment, you were a brave, courageous woman."

The derringer wavered uncertainly.

Reaching out, Longarm gently disengaged the weapon from her gloved hand, them emptied the two cartridges onto the carpet, after which he tossed the weapon onto an upholstered chair.

"But . . . !" she said feebly. "I promised myself . . . !"

He took her in his arms and kissed her, hard and long. When he finished, she sagged gratefully in his arms. Then he lifted her and carried her over to the bed and proceeded to undress her. She smiled dreamily up into his face, her arms about his neck.

"Mmm . . ." she purred. "When I get through with you, maybe you'll wish I *had* pulled the trigger."

"Maybe," he allowed, "but it's a chance I'm willing to take."

By that time she was completely naked under him, and as her swift hands began unbuttoning his fly, they spoke no more.

Their lips were too busy for talking.

Watch for

LONGARM IN THE BITTERROOTS

eighty-second novel in the bold
LONGARM series from Jove

coming in October!